if she saw

(a kate wise mystery—book 2)

blake pierce

ISBN: 978-1-64029-689-3

BOOKS BY BLAKE PIERCE

A JESSIE HUNT PSYCHOLOGICAL SUSPENSE SERIES
THE PERFECT WIFE (Book #1)
THE PERFECT BLOCK (Book #2)
THE PERFECT HOUSE (Book #3)

CHLOE FINE PSYCHOLOGICAL SUSPENSE SERIES
NEXT DOOR (Book #1)
A NEIGHBOR'S LIE (Book #2)

KATE WISE MYSTERY SERIES
IF SHE KNEW (Book #1)
IF SHE SAW (Book #2)

THE MAKING OF RILEY PAIGE SERIES
WATCHING (Book #1)
WAITING (Book #2)
LURING (Book #3)

RILEY PAIGE MYSTERY SERIES
ONCE GONE (Book #1)
ONCE TAKEN (Book #2)
ONCE CRAVED (Book #3)
ONCE LURED (Book #4)
ONCE HUNTED (Book #5)
ONCE PINED (Book #6)
ONCE FORSAKEN (Book #7)
ONCE COLD (Book #8)
ONCE STALKED (Book #9)
ONCE LOST (Book #10)
ONCE BURIED (Book #11)
ONCE BOUND (Book #12)
ONCE TRAPPED (Book #13)
ONCE DORMANT (book #14)

MACKENZIE WHITE MYSTERY SERIES
BEFORE HE KILLS (Book #1)
BEFORE HE SEES (Book #2)
BEFORE HE COVETS (Book #3)
BEFORE HE TAKES (Book #4)
BEFORE HE NEEDS (Book #5)
BEFORE HE FEELS (Book #6)

PROLOGUE

Growing up, Olivia never thought she'd see a day when she was actually *glad* to be home. Like most teens, she'd spent her high school years dreaming of getting away from home, of going to college and starting a life on her own. She'd followed through on her plan, getting out of Whip Springs, Virginia, and attending the University of Virginia. She was in her junior year now, heading into a summer that would be ripe with job opportunities and, by the end of the summer, an apartment search. Olivia enjoyed living on campus, but as a senior she figured it was time to live elsewhere in the city.

For now, though, it was a full month back with her parents in Whip Springs. And she knew her high school self would never forgive her for the relief and surge of love she felt as she pulled into her parents' driveway. They lived just off of a secondary road in Whip Springs—a sleepy little central Virginia town with a population of less than five thousand that was surrounded by forest on all sides, plus a stretch of forest that ran through most of Whip Springs.

It was beginning to get dark when she pulled into the driveway. She had fully expected her mother to have turned the porch light on for her, but there was no glow lighting up the front door. Her mom knew she was arriving this afternoon; they'd discussed it on the phone two days ago and Olivia had even texted three hours ago to tell her she was on the way.

Sure, her mother had not texted back, which was unlike her. But Olivia figured she was probably working overtime to make Olivia's childhood bedroom presentable and forgot to return her text.

As Olivia got closer to the house, she noted that not only was the porch light not on, it seemed as if every single light in the house was turned off. She knew they were home, though. Both of their cars were parked in the driveway, her mother's car parked right behind her father's truck, just like they had been doing for as long as Olivia could remember.

If these cheeseballs are trying to throw me some sort of surprise welcome home party, I might just cry, Olivia thought as she parked beside her mother's car.

She popped the trunk and got her luggage out, just two suitcases but one of which seemed to weigh a ton. She hefted them up the sidewalk and toward the porch. It had been almost a year since she had been back here for a visit; she'd nearly forgotten how absolutely secluded the place felt. The closest neighbors were less than a quarter of a mile away, but the trees surrounding the property made it feel like the house was completely isolated...especially when compared to the crowded dorm spaces back at school.

She wrestled the suitcases up the porch steps and then reached out to ring the doorbell. When she did, she noticed that the door was partially open.

Suddenly, the lack of light from inside seemed sinister—like an alarm of sorts. "Mom? Dad?" she called out as she slowly reached out and opened the door with her foot.

It swung open, revealing the foyer and small hallway that she knew so well. The house was indeed dark but as she stepped inside against the advisement of her growing fear, she was instantly put at ease. From elsewhere in the house, she heard the television—the familiar *dings* and applause of *Wheel of Fortune*, a staple in their home from as far back as Olivia could remember.

As she neared the end of the hallway and approached the living room, she saw the wheel on the TV, which was mounted above the fireplace, a very large screen indeed, making it seem as if Pat Sajak was right there in the living room.

"Hey, guys," Olivia said, looking around the darkened living room. "Thanks so much for helping me with my stuff. Leaving the door cracked open was a—"

It was meant as a joke but when the words hung in her throat, there was nothing funny about it.

Her mother was on the couch. She could have very well been asleep and nothing more than that if it weren't for all the blood. It was all over her chest and soaked into the couch. There was so much of it that Olivia's mind couldn't quite comprehend it at first. Seeing it to the sounds of the clacking of the *Wheel of Fortune* wheel made it somehow even harder to comprehend.

"Mom..."

Olivia felt as if her heart had stopped. She backed slowly away as the reality of what she was seeing sank in. She felt like a small part of her mind had come unhinged and was floating off into space somewhere.

Another word formed on her tongue—*Dad*—as she backed slowly away.

But that's when she saw him. He was right there, on the floor. He was lying just in front of the coffee table and he had just as much blood on him as her mother had. He was lying face down, motionless. But it looked like he was in a crawling position of sorts, as if he had tried to get away. As she took it all in, Olivia saw what looked to be at least six very visible stab wounds in his back.

She suddenly understood why her mother had not answered her text. Her mother was dead. Her father, too.

She felt a scream rising into her throat as she did her best to unlock her legs. She knew that whoever did this might still be here. That thought did it—it brought the scream out, it brought the tears on, and it unlocked her legs.

Olivia dashed out of the house and ran—and ran—and didn't stop running until her screams finally caught in her throat.

CHAPTER ONE

It was funny how quickly Kate Wise's attitude had changed. When she had spent a year in retirement, she'd done everything she could to avoid gardening. Gardening, knitting, bridge clubs—and even book clubs—she had avoided like the plague. They had all seemed like cliché things that retired women did.

But a few months back in the FBI saddle had done something to her. She was not so naïve to think that it had reinvented her. No, it had simply reinvigorated her. She had purpose again, a reason to look forward to the next day.

So maybe that's why she found it okay that she had *now* resorted to gardening as a pastime. It wasn't relaxing, as she had thought it would be. If anything, it made her anxious; why put the time and energy into planting something if you were working against the weather to make sure it stayed alive? Still, there was a joy in it—putting something into the ground and seeing the fruits of it over time.

She'd started with flowers—daisies and bougainvilleas at first—and then went on to planting a little veggie garden in the back right corner of her yard. That's where she was currently mounding dirt over a tomato plant and slowly coming to the realization that she had not had any interest in gardening until she had become a grandmother.

She wondered if it had something to do with the evolution of her nurturing nature. She'd had friends and books tell her that there was something different about being a grandmother—something that a woman never truly tapped into while serving as a mother.

Her daughter, Melissa, had assured her that she had been a good mother. It was an assurance that Kate needed from time to time, given the way she had spent her career. She had admittedly put career over family for far too long and she counted herself lucky that Melissa had not ever resented her for it—except for a period after she had lost her father.

Ah, the one downside to gardening, Kate thought as she got to her feet and dusted off her hands and knees. *Thoughts tend to wander. And when that happens, the past starts creeping in, uninvited.*

4

She left the garden, walking across the backyard of her Richmond, Virginia, home and to the back porch. She was careful to kick off her dirt-smeared Keds at the back door. She also dropped her gloves beside them, not wanting to get any dirt in the house. She'd spent the last two days getting the house clean. She was babysitting Michelle, her granddaughter, tonight and even though Melissa wasn't a neat freak, Kate wanted to have the place sparkling clean. It had been almost thirty years since she'd been in the company of a baby and she didn't want to take any chances.

She glanced at the clock and frowned. She was expecting company in fifteen minutes. That was yet another negative aspect of gardening: time easily slipped away from you.

She freshened up in the bathroom and then went to the kitchen to put a fresh pot of coffee on. It was about halfway through percolating when the doorbell rang. She answered right away, happy as always to see the two women she had been spending a few hours with at least twice a week over the last year and a half or so.

Jane Patterson stepped through the doorway first, carrying a plate of pastries. They were homemade Danishes and had won the Carytown Cooks contest for two years straight. Clarissa James came in behind her with a large bowl of freshly sliced fruit. They were both dressed in cute outfits that would work either at a brunch at a friend's house or casual shopping—which was something they both did quite a bit of.

"You've been gardening again, haven't you?" Clarissa asked as they set their food down in the kitchen island.

"How can you tell?" Kate asked.

Clarissa pointed to Kate's hair, just below the shoulders where it came to a tapered end. Kate reached back and found that she had missed a bit of stray dirt that had somehow ended up in her hair. Clarissa and Jane chuckled at this as Jane took the plastic wrap off of her Danishes.

"Laugh all you want," Kate said. "You won't be when those tomato vines are loaded down."

It was a Friday morning, which automatically made it a good one. The three women situated themselves around Kate's kitchen island, sitting on barstools and eating their brunch and drinking coffee. And while the company, the food, and the coffee were all good, it was still hard to overlook the missing piece.

Debbie Meade was no longer a part of the group. After her daughter had died, one of three victims of a killer Kate had taken down in the end, Debbie and her husband, Jim, had moved. They were living somewhere out near the beach in North Carolina.

Debbie would send pictures of the coast from time to time, just to jokingly rub it in. They had been living there for two months now and seemed to be happy—to be moving on from the tragedy.

The conversation was mostly light and pleasant. Jane talked about how her husband was eyeing retirement next year and had already started planning to write a book. Clarissa shared news about both of her kids, now in their mid-twenties, and how they'd both recently received promotions.

"Speaking of kids," Clarissa said, "how is Melissa doing? She loving motherhood?"

"Oh yes," Kate said. "She's absolutely insane about her little baby girl. A little baby girl that I will be babysitting tonight, in fact."

"First time?" Jane asked.

"Yes. It's the first time Melissa and Terry are going somewhere without the baby. Like an actual overnight thing."

"Has Grandma Mode kicked in yet?" Clarissa asked.

"I don't know," Kate said with a smile. "I guess we'll find out tonight."

"You know," Jane said, "you could go back in time and babysit like I used to in high school. I'd bring my boyfriend over with me and as soon as the kids went to bed…"

"That's pretty disturbing," Kate said.

"Do you think Allen would be up for it, though?" Clarissa asked.

"I don't know," Kate answered, trying to imagine Allen with a baby. They had been dating seriously ever since Kate and her new partner, DeMarco, had wrapped the serial case right here in Richmond—the same case that had taken Debbie Meade's daughter. There had been no real talk of the future; they hadn't slept together yet and rarely got physical at all. She was enjoying her time with him, though, but the thought of bringing him into the grandmother part of her life made her uncomfortable.

"Things still going well with you two?" Clarissa asked.

"I think so. The whole dating thing still seems weird to me. I'm too old to date, you know?"

"Hell no," Jane said. "Don't get me wrong…I love my husband, my kids, and my life in general. But I'd give anything to be back on that dating scene for just a while, you know? I miss it. Meeting new people, sharing firsts…"

"Yeah, I guess that *is* pretty nice," Kate conceded. "Allen finds the idea of dating strange, too. We have fun together but it's…it gets sort of weird when things start leaning towards the romantic end of things."

"Blah blah," Clarissa said. "But do you think of him as your boyfriend?"

"Are we really having this conversation?" Kate asked, starting to feel herself blushing a bit.

"Yes," Clarissa said. "Us old married ladies need to live vicariously through you."

"And that also goes for your sort-of job," Jane said. "How's that going?"

"No calls for about two weeks, and the last one was just to help with some research. Sorry, girls…it's not as adventurous as you're hoping it is."

"So are you back to being retired?" Clarissa asked.

"Basically. It's complicated."

That comment ended the questioning as they delved back into local topics—upcoming movies, a music festival in town, construction on the interstate, and so on. But Kate's mind had gotten snagged on the topic of work. It was comforting to know that the bureau was still considering her as a resource but she had been hoping for a more active role after she had tied things up with the last case. But so far, she'd only heard from Deputy Director Duran a single time, and that was to get a performance review on DeMarco.

She knew how strange it seemed to her friends that she was still technically an active agent while also leaning into her role as a grandmother. Hell, it was strange to her as well. Throw in a slowly blossoming relationship with Allen and she supposed her life *was* quite interesting to them.

Honestly, she counted herself lucky. She'd be fifty-six years old at the end of the month and she knew that many women her age would be envious of the life she lived. She always told herself this when she felt the pressing need to be more active at work. And some days, it worked.

And as it just so happened, with her granddaughter coming to visit for the first time since her birth, today was one of those days.

***

One thing that made it difficult to balance her new role as grandmother with her desire to get her hands deep into another case was trying to think like a grandmother. That afternoon, she left her house and walked down to some of the thrifty little shops in the

Carytown district of Richmond. She felt like she had to get Michelle a gift to celebrate her first overnight stay at Grandma's house.

It was hard to push sidearms and suspects aside to focus on stuffed animals and onesies instead. But as she checked out a few shops, it became somewhat easier. She found that she actually enjoyed shopping for her granddaughter, even though she wasn't even two months old yet and would, honestly, not care about any gift she got. She found it hard not to snatch up every cute thing she found and buy it. After all, wasn't it the responsibility of a grandmother to spoil her grandchildren?

As she paid for her purchases at the third shop she visited, she received a text. She wasted no time in checking it. Over the last few weeks, she'd had a small hope every time she got a call or a text, thinking it might Duran or someone else within the bureau. She mentally scolded herself when she was disappointed to find that it was not the bureau, but Allen. Once she got over the sting of not being called upon by the bureau again, she realized that she was happy to hear from him—was *always* happy to hear from him, in fact.

"Allen, you have to help me," she joked as she answered the phone. "I'm shopping for Michelle and everything I see, I want to buy for her. Is that normal?"

"I don't know," Allen said. "Neither of my sons have settled down and made me a grandpa yet."

"Take it from me. Start saving up."

Allen chuckled, a sound that Kate was growing to like quite a bit. "So tonight's the big night, huh?"

"It is. And I know I raised a kid already and I know what to expect, but I'm a little terrified."

"Ah, you'll be great. You want to talk terrified…I'm going out with my boys for drinks tonight. And I haven't had more than two drinks in a single sitting in about five years."

"Have fun with that."

"I was wondering if you might want to get together tomorrow for dinner. We can share our survival stories of tonight."

"I'd like that. You want to come by my place at seven or so?"

"Sounds like a plan. You have fun tonight. Is little Michelle sleeping through the night yet?"

"I don't believe so."

"Ouch," Allen said, and ended the call.

Kate pocketed her phone, juggling her bags of purchases as she did. She smiled in spite of herself. She was standing in the sunshine in her favorite part of town, having just gone shopping for a two-month-old granddaughter, whom she was babysitting tonight. Given the way her day was going, did she *really* want the bureau to call at all?

She was walking back to her home—a three-block walk from where she had taken Allen's call—when she saw a little girl with a *My Little Pony* T-shirt. She was walking with her mother hand in hand, just a few feet ahead of her, traveling in their direction. She was five or six years old, her blonde hair up in a ponytail only a mother's care could create. She had blue eyes and a sharp end to her nose that looked rather pixie-like. And it was that feature that sent a spike of despair through Kate's heart.

An image flashed through her mind, a little girl who looked almost identical to this one. But in this image, the little girl had dirt and grime on her face, and she was crying. The lights of police cars flashed behind her.

The image was so strong that it caused Kate to stop walking for a moment. She tore her eyes away from the girl, not wanting to appear creepy or strange. She clung to that image in her head and did her best to find the memory associated with it. It came to her gradually and when it did, it unrolled itself slowly, as if she were reading the case report.

Five-year-old girl, found three days after reported missing. Stored in a fishing cabin in Arkansas with the dead bodies of her parents. The parents were the fifth and sixth victims of a serial killer that had terrorized Arkansas for the better part of four months...a killer Kate had eventually taken down, but only after he had claimed a total of nine people.

Kate was aware that she was suddenly standing as still as a statue on the street but couldn't seem to move. That case had haunted her for a while. So many dead ends, so many false leads. She had been running around in circles, unable to find the killer while he continued to add to his body count. God only knew what he had planned for that little girl.

But you saved her, she told herself. *In the end, you saved her.*

Kate slowly started to walk again. It was not the first time a random image from her past work had slammed itself across her mind and caused her to zone out. Sometimes they came casually, albeit out of nowhere. But there were other times when they came on strong and fast, like a post-traumatic stress flashback.

The image of the girl from Arkansas was somewhere in between. And Kate was thankful for that. That particular case had nearly caused her to step down as an agent back in 2009. It had been soul-shattering, enough for Kate to request two weeks off from work. And all of a sudden, for just a split second while walking back home with gifts for her granddaughter in her hand, Kate felt like she had been pushed back in time.

Nearly ten years had passed since she had rescued that girl. Kate wondered where she was—wondered if she had outlived the trauma.

"Ma'am?"

Kate blinked, jumping a bit at the sound of an unfamiliar voice in front of her. There was a teenage boy standing in front her. He looked concerned, as if he wasn't sure if he should be standing there or running away.

"Are you okay?" he asked. "You look…I don't know. Sick. Like you're about to pass out or something."

"No," Kate said, shaking her head. "I'm good. Thanks."

The kid nodded and carried on his way. Kate started walking forward again, ripped out of some hole in the past that she assumed had not yet quite closed up. And as she drew closer and closer to home, she started to wonder just how many of those holes from her past had been left uncovered.

And if the ghosts of her past would continue to haunt her until she, too, became a ghost.

CHAPTER TWO

Kate spent the next hour or so tidying up the house, even though she had already done so before leaving to go shopping. It made her feel off to be so anxious to have Michelle coming to her house. Melissa had lived in this house during her high school years so when she came to visit (which wasn't often enough in Kate's opinion), Kate didn't feel the need for the place to be spotless. So why was she so concerned about how it looked for a two-month-old?

Maybe it's some odd kind of grandmother nesting, she thought while she scrubbed the sink in the powder room...a room she was well aware that her granddaughter would not even see, much less actually use.

As she rinsed the sink out, her doorbell rang. She was flooded with an excitement that she had not quite been ready for. She was smiling from ear to ear when she answered the door. Melissa stood on the other side, carrying Michelle in her car seat. The baby was fast asleep, a thick blanket tucked around her legs.

"Hey, Mom," Melissa said as she stepped into the house. She took a quick look around and rolled her eyes. "How much did you clean today?"

"I plead the fifth," Kate said as she gave her daughter a hug.

Melissa set the car seat down carefully on the floor and slowly unbuckled Michelle. She picked her up and handed her softly to Kate. It had been almost a full week since Kate had visited Melissa and Terry, but when she took Michelle into her arms, it felt like much longer.

"What do you and Terry have planned for tonight?" Kate asked.

"Not much, really," Melissa said. "And that's the beauty of it. We're going to go out for dinner and drinks. Maybe some dancing. Also, we changed our minds about asking you to watch her overnight because we realized we're not quite ready for that. The unbroken sleep is much needed, but I just can't be away from her for that long."

"Oh, I think I can understand that," Kate said. "You guys go out and enjoy yourselves."

Melissa shrugged the diaper bag from her shoulder and set it by the car seat. "Everything you need is in here. She's going to want to eat again in about an hour and she'd going to fight sleep. Terry thinks it's cute but I think it's of the devil. If she gets gassy, there are gas drops in the back pocket and—"

"Lissa…we'll be fine. I *have* raised a child, you know. She turned out pretty good, too."

Melissa smiled and surprised Kate by giving her a quick kiss on the cheek. "Thanks, Mom. I'll pick her up around eleven or so. Is that too late?"

"Nope, that's perfect."

Melissa gave one final look to her baby, a look that made Kate's heart swell. She could remember being a mother and having that internal feeling of love fill her—a love than translated to the sheer will of doing anything and everything to ensure this human you'd created would be safe.

"If you need anything, call me," Melissa said, though she was still looking at Michelle and not Kate.

"I will. Now *go*. Have fun."

Melissa finally turned away and headed out the door. As she closed it, little Michelle stirred awake in Kate's arms. She gave her grandmother a sleepy little smile and let out a tiny yawn.

"So what do we do now?" Kate asked.

The question was playfully directed at Michelle but she felt a weight behind it that made her wonder if she was simply voicing a rhetorical question to herself. Her daughter was grown up now, with a daughter of her own. Now here she was, nearing fifty-six and with her first grandchild in her arms. So…*what do we do now?*

She thought about that pull to return to work in any capacity and, for perhaps the first time, it felt small.

Smaller even than the little girl she now held in her arms.

***

By eight o'clock that night, Kate was wondering if Melissa and Terry had simply managed to create the most well-behaved baby in recorded history. Not once did Michelle cry or even get fussy. She was simply content to be held. After two hours in Kate's arms, Michelle nodded off to sleep. Kate carefully placed Michelle on the center of her queen-sized bed and then stood at the doorway for a moment to watch her granddaughter sleep.

She wasn't sure how long she had been standing there when her phone buzzed from the kitchen table behind her. She had to tear her eyes away from Michelle but managed to get to the phone within a few seconds. The single buzz meant that it was a text rather than a call and she was not at all surprised to see that it was Melissa.

How's she doing? Melissa asked.

Unable to resist, Kate smiled and responded: **I limited her to just three beers. She went out with some guy on a motorcycle about an hour ago. I told her to be back by 11.**

The response came quickly: **Oh, you're not funny at all.**

The back-and-forth banter made her nearly as happy as the sleeping baby in her bedroom. After her father died, Melissa had become withdrawn—especially toward Kate. She'd blamed Kate's work for her father's death and even though she had come to understand that was not the case later on in life, there were times when Kate felt that Melissa still resented the time she had spent in the bureau after his death. Oddly enough, though, Melissa had shown some interest in pursuing a career in the FBI herself...despite a less-than-positive attitude about the events of the last year concerning her mother's interrupted retirement.

Still smiling, Kate took her phone into the bedroom and snapped a quick picture of Michelle. She sent it to Melissa and then, after some thought, she also sent it to Allen, only his had the message: **Partied out!**

She found herself wishing he was there with her. She found herself feeling this quite often as of late. She was not naïve enough to think she loved him, but she could see herself falling *in* love with him if things kept going the way they were. She missed him when he wasn't around and whenever he kissed her, it made her feel about twenty years younger.

She found herself smiling yet again when Allen responded with a picture of his own. It was a selfie of him with two younger men who looked exactly like him—his sons, presumably.

As she studied the picture, her phone rang in her hands. The name that appeared on the screen sent a flurry of excitement through her that she was unable to stop.

Deputy Director Vince Duran was calling her. This would have caused a stir of excitement regardless, but the fact that it was after eight o'clock on a Friday night set off alarm bells in her head—alarm bells that she enjoyed the sound of.

She took a moment, still staring at little Michelle, and then answered. "This is Kate Wise," she said, keeping her excitement in check.

"Wise, it's Duran. Is this a bad time?"

"It's not the absolute best, but that's okay," she answered. "Is everything okay?"

"That depends. I'm calling to see if you'd be interested in taking on a case."

"Are we talking a cold case like we've been discussing?"

"No. This one…well, it looks and feels like one you cracked rather quickly back in ninety-six. As it stands, we've got four bodies at two different sites in Whip Springs, Virginia. Looks like the murders occurred no more than two days apart. Right now, Virginia State Police are running the scene but I've spoken to them. If you want the case, it's yours. But you'd have to move now."

"I don't think I can," she said. "I've got a commitment I need to keep." Looking at Michelle, this was easy to say. But nearly every nerve in her body fought against her newly acquired grandmother instincts.

"Well, listen to the specs anyway, would you? The murders are married couples, one in their early fifties, the other in their early sixties. The most recent were the fifty-somethings. Their daughter discovered their bodies when she came home from college earlier today. The murders occurred within thirty miles of one another, one in Whip Springs and the other one just outside of Roanoke."

"Couples? Any link between them other than they were married?"

"Not yet. But all four bodies were cut up pretty badly. The killer is using a knife. Making it slow and methodical. As far as I'm concerned, it points to another couple going down within two days or so."

"Yeah, it sounds like a serial in the making," Kate said.

She thought back to the case in 1996 that Duran had mentioned. In the end, a crazed woman who had been working as a nanny had taken the lives of three couples within the span of just two days. It turned out that she had worked for all three of the couples within a ten-year period. Kate had apprehended the woman when she was on the way to kill a fourth couple and then, according to her testimony, herself.

Was she *really* going to say no to this? After the intense flashback she'd had today, could she truly pass up another opportunity at stopping a killer?

"How long do I have to think about it?" she asked.

"I'll give you an hour. No more than that. I need someone on this now. And I thought you and DeMarco could work well on it. One hour, Wise…sooner if you can."

Before she could give an *OK* or a *thanks,* Duran ended the call. He was typically warm and friendly, but when he did not get his way he could be very irritable.

As quietly as she could, she went to the bed and sat down on the edge. She watched Michelle sleeping, the gentle rise and fall of her chest so slow and methodical. She could clearly remember Melissa being this small and had no idea where the time had gone. And that was where her problem sprung from: she felt that she had missed so much of her life as a mother and wife because of her job but she felt a strong duty to it nonetheless. Especially when she knew that she could be out there right now, doing her part to bring a killer to justice.

What kind of a person would she be if she turned the offer down, leaving Duran to choose another agent who might not have the same skillsets as she did?

But what kind of grandmother and mother was she being if she had to call Melissa, telling her to come pick up her daughter early and end her night out because the FBI had come calling again?

Kate stared at Michelle for about five minutes, even lying down next to her and placing her hand on the baby's chest just to feel her breathe. And seeing that little flicker of life, of a life that had not yet learned about the kinds of evil that existed in the world, made the decision much easier for Kate.

Frowning for the first time that day, Kate picked up the phone and called Melissa.

***

Once, when Melissa was sixteen, she'd snuck a boy into her room late at night when Kate and Michael were already asleep. Kate had stirred awake at some noise (which she later found out was likely someone's knee hitting the wall in Melissa's bedroom) and went up to investigate. When she opened her daughter's door and found her topless with a boy in her bed, she had thrown him off the bed and screamed at him to get out.

The fury in Melissa's eyes that night was dwarfed by what Kate saw in her daughter's stare as she buckled Michelle into the car seat at 9:30—just a little over an hour after Duran had called her about the case in Roanoke.

"This is messed up, Mom," she said.

"Lissa, I'm so sorry. But what the hell was I supposed to do?"

"Well, from what I understand, people actually *stay* retired once they've retired. Maybe try that!"

15

"It's not that easy," Kate argued.

"Oh, I know, Mom," Melissa said. "It never was with you."

"That's not fair…"

"And don't think I'm just pissed because you cut my *one night* to relax short. I don't care about that. I'm not *that* selfish. Unlike *some* people. I'm pissed because your job—which you were supposed to be done with over a year ago, mind you—continues to win over your family. Even after everything…after *Dad*…"

"Lissa, let's not do this."

Melissa picked up the car seat with a softness that was not present in her voice or her body's strained posture.

"I agree," Melissa spat. "Let's not."

And with that, she walked out of the front door, slamming it behind her.

Kate reached out for the doorknob but stopped. What was she going to do? Was she going to continue this argument outside, in the yard? Besides, she knew Melissa well. After a few days, she'd cool down and would actually listen to Kate's side of the story. She might even accept her mother's apology.

Kate felt like a traitor as she picked up her cell phone. After she'd called Duran, he informed her that he'd planned on her showing up for the case anyway. As it stood, he had someone from the Virginia State Police lined up to meet with her and DeMarco at 4:30 in the morning down in Whip Springs. As for DeMarco, she had left DC half an hour ago with an agency car. She'd be at Kate's house sometime around midnight. Kate realized she could have easily kept Michelle until the originally planned on eleven o'clock and avoided the confrontation with Melissa. But she couldn't dwell on that now.

The suddenness of it all had taken Kate slightly off guard. Even though the last case she had taken had seemed to come out of nowhere, it had at least had some sort of stable structure to it. But it had been quite a while since she had been assigned a case at such an hour. It was daunting but she was also very excited—excited enough to be able to momentarily push Melissa's anger toward her to the back of her mind.

Still, as she packed a bag while waiting for DeMarco to arrive, a stinging thought pierced her. *And it's that right there—your ability to push everything to the side for the sake of the job—that caused so much trouble between the two of you in the first place.*

But that thought too was easily pushed to the side.

CHAPTER THREE

One of the many things Kate had learned about DeMarco during their last case was that she was punctual. It was a trait she was reminded of when she heard a knock on her door at 12:10.

I don't remember the last time I had a visitor this late, she thought. *College, maybe?*

She walked to the door, carrying her single packed bag with her. Yet when she answered the door, she saw that DeMarco had no intention of just rushing out to drive to the crime scene.

"At the risk of seeming rude, I really need to use your bathroom," DeMarco said. "Chugging two Cokes to stay awake for the ride was a *bad* idea."

Kate smiled and stepped aside to let DeMarco in. Given the speed and urgency Duran had instilled in her during their phone calls, DeMarco's abruptness was the kind of unintentional comic relief she needed. It also made her feel comfortable to know that even after almost two months apart, she and DeMarco were picking back up on the same comfort level they had shared before parting ways after the last case.

DeMarco came out of the bathroom a few minutes later with an embarrassed smile on her face.

"And good morning to you," Kate said. Maybe it was because of the caffeine intake, but DeMarco did not seem any worse for the wear, apparently not fazed by the early hour.

DeMarco looked at her watch and nodded. "Yeah, I suppose it *is* morning."

"When did you get the call?" Kate asked.

"Around eight or nine, I guess. I would have left earlier, but Duran wanted to make one hundred percent sure you were on board."

"Sorry about that," Kate said. "I was babysitting my granddaughter for the first time."

"Oh no. Wise...that sucks. I'm sorry this is screwing with that."

Kate shrugged and waved it away. "It'll be fine. You ready to get going?"

"Yeah. I fielded a few calls on the way over while this was being managed by the guys back in DC. We're scheduled to meet with one of the guys from Virginia State PD at four thirty at the Nash residence."

"The Nash residence?" Kate asked.

"The most recent couple to be murdered."

They fell into step together back toward the front door. As they made their way out, Kate turned the living room light off and picked up her bag. She was excited about what might lie ahead, but she also felt like she was leaving her home rather irrationally. After all, just a few hours ago, her two-month-old granddaughter had been snoozing on her bed. And now here she was, about to drive straight to a murder scene.

She saw the standard bureau sedan parked in front of her house, right along the curb. It looked surreal, but also inviting.

"You want to drive?" DeMarco asked.

"Sure," Kate said, wondering if the younger agent was offering the role as a show of respect or because she simply wanted a break from driving.

Kate got behind the wheel while DeMarco pulled up directions to the location of the most recent murder. It was in the town of Whip Springs, Virginia, a little hole-in-the wall town situated at the base of the Blue Ridge Mountains just outside of Roanoke. They spent only a little time on small talk—Kate filling DeMarco in on how it felt to be a grandmother, while DeMarco remained mostly silent, mentioning only yet another failed relationship after her girlfriend left her. This came as a surprise, as Kate had not pegged DeMarco as being gay. If anything, it showed her that she really needed to spend some more time getting to know the woman who was more or less her partner. Punctuality, she had picked up on. Homosexuality, she had missed. What the hell did that say about her as a partner?

As the crime scene drew closer, DeMarco read over the reports that Duran had sent them pertaining to the case. As she read them, Kate kept looking for any traces of the sun breaking the horizon but saw none.

"Two older couples," DeMarco said. "Sorry…one in their late fifties…so no offense."

"None taken," Kate said, not sure if this was DeMarco's weird attempt at humor.

"At first glance, they appear to have nothing in common, other than location. The first scene was right in the heart of Roanoke and this most recent one was no more than thirty miles away, in Whip

Springs. There appear to be no signs that the husband or the wife were the preliminary targets. Each murder was gruesome and a little overdone, indicating that the killer enjoys it."

"And that typically points to someone who feels that they have been wronged by the victims in some cases," Kate pointed out. "That or some twisted psychological craving for violence and bloodshed."

"The most recent victims, the Nashes, had been married for twenty-four years. They have two children, one who lives in San Diego and another who is currently attending UVA. She's the one who discovered the bodies when she came home yesterday."

"What about the other couple?" Kate asked. "They have any kids?"

"Not according to the reports."

Kate mulled all of this over and for reasons she could not grasp, found herself thinking of the little girl she had passed on the street earlier in the day. Or, rather, the flashback that little girl had spurred up in her mind.

When they arrived at the Nash residence, the horizon had finally started to catch some of the light from the rising but still absent sun. It peeked through the tree line that surrounded most of the Nashes' yard. In that light, they could see a single car parked in front of the house. A man stood propped against the hood, smoking a cigarette and holding a cup of coffee.

"You guys Wise and DeMarco?" the man asked.

"That's us," Kate said, stepping forward and showing her ID. "Who are you?"

"Palmetto, with Virginia State PD. Forensics. I got the call a few hours ago that you two would be taking the case. Figured I might as well be here to hand off what I have. Which, by the way, isn't much."

Palmetto took one final drag from his cigarette and tossed it to the ground, snuffing it out with his foot. "The bodies have obviously been moved and there was very little evidence found anywhere. But come on inside anyway. It's...eye opening."

Palmetto spoke with the emotionless tone of a man who had been doing this for quite some time. He led them up the Nashes' sidewalk and onto the porch. When he opened the door and led them inside, Kate could smell it: the smell of a crime scene where a lot of blood had been spilled. There was something chemical to it, not just the coppery smell of blood, but of recent movement and people with rubber gloves looking over the scene recently.

Palmetto turned each light on they made their way into the house—through the foyer, down a hallway, and into the living room. In the bright glare of overhead lights, Kate saw the first splotch of blood on the hardwood floor. And then another and another.

Palmetto led them to the front of the couch, pointing to the bloodstains like a man simply confirming the fact that water is indeed wet.

"The bodies were here, one on the couch and one on the floor. It appeared that the mother was killed first, probably from the cut to her neck, although one did seem to land pretty close to her heart, but through the back. It's theorized that there was a struggle with the father. There was bruising on his forearms, some blood coming out of his mouth, and the coffee table had been knocked askew."

"Any early ideas on the time that passed between the murders and the daughter discovering them?" Kate asked.

"No more than a day," Palmetto answered. "And it was probably more like twelve or sixteen hours. I'm sure the coroner will have something a little more concrete at some point today."

"Anything else of note?" DeMarco asked.

"Yes, actually. It's a piece of evidence…just one single piece." He reached into the inner pocket of his thin jacket and pulled out a small evidence baggie. "I kept this. Got permission, so don't get all spooked. I figured you'd want to take it and run. It's the only evidence we found, but it's pretty unnerving."

He offered the clear plastic baggie to Kate. She took it and eyed the contents inside. From what she could tell, it was a simple piece of cloth, about six-by-three inches. It was thick, blue in color, and had a fluffy texture to it. The entire right side of it was stained in blood.

"Where was this found?" Kate asked.

"Stuffed into the mother's mouth. It was pushed deep down there, almost down her throat."

Kate held it up to the light. "Any idea where it came from?" she asked.

"No idea. Looks to be just a random scrap."

But Kate wasn't so sure. In fact, her grandmother's intuition started storming to the front. This was not some random piece of fabric. No…it was soft, it was light blue, and looked to be quite fluffy.

This was part of a blanket. Perhaps a child's security blanket.

"You holding any other surprise evidence for us?" DeMarco asked.

20

"No, that's it out of me," Palmetto said, already heading back for the door. "If you ladies need any help from this point on, feel free to give us a call at the State PD."

Kate and DeMarco shared an annoyed look behind his back. Without having to say anything, they each knew that the term *you ladies* had pissed the other off.

"Well, that was brief," DeMarco said as Palmetto gave them a noncommittal wave from the front door.

"Just as well," Kate said. "This way we can start looking the case over with our own eyes, without the influence of what anyone else has found."

"You think we need to speak to the daughter next?"

"Probably. And then we'll look into the first crime scene and see if we can find anything there. Hopefully we'll find someone who's a bit more sociable than our friend Palmetto."

They headed back out of the house, turning off the lights as they went. As they headed back outside, the sun finally peeking out from the edge of the world, Kate carefully placed what she thought was a scrap of a child's blanket into her pocket and could not help but think of her granddaughter sleeping under a similar blanket.

Walking toward the sun did nothing to suppress the chill that crept through her.

CHAPTER FOUR

Breakfast consisted of a Panera Bread drive-thru in Roanoke. It was there, while waiting in the small early-morning line, that DeMarco placed several calls to set up a meeting with Olivia Nash, daughter of the recently slayed couple. She was currently staying with her aunt in Roanoke and was, by her aunt's own words, an absolute wreck.

After getting the address and approval from the aunt, they headed for the aunt's house just after seven o'clock. The early hour was not an issue because, according to the aunt, Olivia had refused to sleep ever since having discovered her parents.

When Kate and DeMarco arrived at the house, the aunt was sitting on the porch. Cami Nash stood when Kate got out of the car but made no move to come meet them. She had a cup of coffee in her hand and the tired look on her face made Kate think it was certainly not the first she had enjoyed this morning.

"Cami Nash?" Kate asked.

"Yeah, that's me," she said.

"First and foremost, please accept my sympathies for your loss," Kate said. "Were you and your brother close?"

"Pretty close, yeah. But right now, I have to look past that. I can't... *grieve* right now because Olivia needs someone. She's not the same person I spoke with on the phone last week. Something in her is broken. I can't even imagine…what it must have been like to find them like that and…"

She trailed off and sipped down some of her coffee very quickly, trying to distract herself from the onslaught of tears that seemed to be rapidly approaching.

"Is she going to be okay to speak with us?" DeMarco asked.

"Maybe for a while. I told her you were coming and she seemed to understand what I meant. That's why I'm meeting you out here before you go in. I feel like I need to tell you that she's a normal, well-rounded young woman. In the state she's in now, though, I didn't want you to think she had some sort of mental issues or something."

"Thanks for that," Kate said. She had seen people absolutely devastated by grief before and it was never a pretty sight. She couldn't help but wonder how much experience DeMarco had with it.

Cami led them into the house. It was as quiet as a tomb inside, the only sound coming from the hum of the air conditioner. Kate noticed that Cami walked slowly, making sure not to make too much noise. Kate followed suit, wondering if Cami was hoping the silence would help Olivia finally fall asleep or if she was simply trying not to alarm the already-fragile young woman in any way.

They entered the living room, where a young woman was half-sitting, half-lying on the couch. Her face was red, her eyes slightly swollen from recently weeping. She looked as if she hadn't slept in about a week rather than just a day or so. When she saw Kate and DeMarco enter, she sat up a bit.

"Hi, Ms. Nash," Kate said. "Thank you for agreeing to meet with us. We're so sorry for your loss."

"It's Olivia, please." Her voice was hoarse and tired—almost as worn out as her eyes seemed to be.

"We'll make this as quick as possible," Kate said. "I understand that you had just come in from college. Do you know if your parents had planned to have anyone else over that day?"

"If they did, I didn't know about it."

"Please forgive me for asking, but do you know if either of your parents had any long-standing grudges with anyone? People they might have considered enemies?"

Olivia shook her head firmly. "Dad was married once before...before he met Mom. But even with his ex-wife, he was on good terms."

Olivia started crying noiselessly. A series of tears slipped from her eyes and she did not bother trying to wipe them away.

"I want to show you something," Kate said. "I don't know if it has any significance to you or not. If it does, it could be quite emotional. Would you be willing to take a look and let us know if it looks familiar to you?"

Olivia looked alarmed, maybe even a little scared. Kate really didn't blame here and almost didn't want to show her the scrap of fabric Palmetto had handed them—the scrap Kate felt certain was part of a blanket or quilt. A bit reluctantly, she pulled it out of her pocket.

She knew right away that Olivia didn't recognize it. There was an immediate sense of relief and confusion on the young woman's face as she looked at the plastic bag and what it held inside.

Olivia shook her head but kept her eyes locked on the clear plastic bag. "No. I don't recognize it. Why?"

"We can't reveal that right now," Kate said. Truthfully, there was nothing unlawful about revealing it to the next of kin...but Kate didn't see the point in traumatizing Olivia Nash any further.

"Do you have any idea who did this?" Olivia asked. She looked lost, like she did not recognize where she was...maybe not even herself. Kate couldn't recall the last time she had seen someone so clearly detached from everything around her.

"Not right now," she said. "But we will keep you posted. And please," she said, looking from Olivia and then to Cami, "contact us if you can think of *anything* that might help."

At that remark, DeMarco withdrew a business card from the inner pocket of her jacket and handed it to Cami.

Perhaps it was the years she had spent in retirement or feeling guilty for having to abandon her post as grandmother last night, but Kate felt awful when she left the room, leaving Olivia Nash to her intense grief. As she and DeMarco made their way out onto the porch, she could hear the young woman let out a low moan of distress.

Kate and DeMarco shared an uneasy glace as they headed to the car. From within her inner pocket, Kate could feel the presence of that scrap of fabric and it suddenly felt very heavy indeed.

CHAPTER FIVE

As Kate left the small town of Whip Springs and headed for Roanoke, DeMarco used her iPad to pull up the case files on the first set of murders. It was nearly an exact copy and paste of the Nash crime scene; a couple had been murdered in their home in a particularly gruesome fashion. Preliminary results turned up no likely suspects and there had been no witnesses.

"Does it say anything about anything left behind in the throats or mouths of either of the victims?" Kate asked.

DeMarco scanned the reports and shook her head. "Not from what I can see. I think it's maybe a—no, wait, here it is. In the coroner's report. The fabric wasn't discovered until yesterday—a day and a half after the bodies were discovered. But yes…the report says that there was a small piece of fabric lodged in the mother's throat."

"Does it give a description?"

"No. I'll give the coroner a call and see if I can get a picture of it."

DeMarco wasted no time, making the call right away. While she was on the phone, Kate tried to think of anything that might be able to link two seemingly random couples, given what had been found in the throats of the females. While Kate had yet to see the piece of fabric that had been taken from the throat of the first female victim, she was fully expecting it to match the one that had been found in the throat of Mrs. Nash.

DeMarco's call was over three minutes later. Seconds after she ended the call, she received a text. She glanced at her phone and said: "We've got a match."

Approaching a stoplight as they inched their way further into the city of Roanoke, Kate looked over to the phone as DeMarco showed it to her. As Kate expected, the fabric was soft and blue in color—an exact match for the one found in the throat of the Nash mother.

"We've got pretty extensive records on both couples, right?" Kate asked.

"Decent, I suppose," she said. "Based on the records and case files we have, there might be *some* stuff missing, but I think we've

25

got quite a bit to go on." She paused here as the GPS app on the iPad dinged. "Turn left at this light," DeMarco said. "The house is half a mile down this next street."

Kate's mental wheels were turning quickly as they neared the first crime scene.

Two married couples, slaughtered in a brutal way. Remnants or scraps of some sort of old blanket found in the throats of the wives…

There were many ways to go with the clues they had been given. But before Kate could focus on a single one and put it together, DeMarco was speaking up.

"Right there," she said, pointing to a small brick house on the right.

Kate pulled up alongside the curb. The house was located on a thin side street, the kind that connected two main roads. It was a quiet street with a few other small houses taking up the space. The street had an almost historic feel to it, the sidewalks faded and cracked, the houses in a similar state.

Faded white letters on the mailbox read LANGLEY. Kate also spotted a decorative L hanging on the front door, made of aged wood. It stood out against the bright yellow of the crime scene tape that hung from the porch railings.

As Kate and DeMarco headed for the front porch, DeMarco half read, half recited the information they had in the reports on the Langley family.

"Scott and Bethany Langley—Scott fifty-nine years of age, Bethany sixty-one. Scott was found dead in the kitchen and Bethany was in the laundry room. They were found by a fifteen-year-old boy who was taking private guitar lessons from Scott. It's estimated that they had only been killed a few hours before the bodies were discovered."

When they entered the Langley residence, Kate stood in the doorway for a moment, taking in the layout of the place. It was a smaller house, but well kept. The front door opened into a very small foyer which then became the living room. From there, a small bar top counter separated the kitchen from the living room. A hallway stood off to the right, leading to the rest of the house.

The layout of the house alone told Kate that the husband had likely been killed first. But from the front door, there was pretty much a clear view into the kitchen. Scott Langley would have had to have been quite busy not to notice someone walking through the front door.

Maybe the killer came in some other way, Kate thought.

They entered the kitchen, where bloodstains still stood out prominently on the laminate floor. A frying pan and a can of cooking spray were sitting by the edge of the stove.

He was about to cook something, Kate thought. *So maybe they were killed right around dinner time.*

DeMarco started for the hallway, and Kate followed her. There was a small room immediately to the left, the door opening to reveal a crowded laundry room. Here, the blood splatter had been much worse. There were bloodstains on the washer, the dryer, the walls, the floor, and on a load of neatly folded clean clothes sitting in a hamper.

With the bodies already removed, there seemed to be very little the Langley residence could offer them. But Kate had one more thing she wanted to check. She walked back out into the living room and looked at the pictures on the walls and atop the entertainment center. She saw the Langleys smiling and happy. In one picture, she saw an older couple with the Langleys posing by the end of a pier at the beach.

"Do we have a breakdown of the Langleys' family life?" Kate asked.

DeMarco, still holding the iPad in her right hand, scrolled through the information and started to read out the details they had. With each one, Kate found that the hunch she had been sitting on for a few minutes was likely true.

"They were married for twenty-five years. Bethany Langley had a sister that died in a car accident twelve years ago and neither of them have any surviving parents. Scott Langley's father passed away recently, just six months ago, from an aggressive form of prostate cancer."

"Any mention of kids?"

"Nope. No kids." DeMarco paused here and seemed to catch on to what Kate was speculating on. "You're thinking about the fabric, right? That it looks sort of like a kid's blanket."

"Yeah, that's what I was thinking. But if the Langleys didn't have kids I don't think there would be any obvious connection to be found."

"I don't know that I've ever seen an *obvious* connection to anything," DeMarco said with a shaky little laugh.

"That's true," Kate said, but she felt like there had to be one here. Even with the seemingly random victims, there were a few things they *did* have in common.

Both couples were both in their mid-to-late fifties, early sixties. Both were married. The wife of each couple had a piece of what appears to be a blanket shoved down her throat.

So yes…there were similarities, but they were leading to no real links. Not yet, anyway.

"Agent DeMarco, do you think you could make a call or two and make sure we can get some office space at the local police department?"

"Already done," she said. "I'm pretty sure Duran handled all of that before we even arrived here."

He thinks he knows me so well, Kate thought, a little irritated. But then, on the other hand, it appeared that he *did* know her pretty damned well.

Kate glanced around the house again, at the pictures, at the bloodstains. She was going to have to get deeper into the details of each couple if she wanted to get anywhere with this. And she was going to need to get some kind of forensic results on the fabric pieces. Given the similarities between the two scenes, she assumed some good old basic research more than anything would uncover some leads and clues.

They returned to the car, Kate again reminded that they had started this day ridiculously early. When she saw that it was just after ten in the morning, she was somewhat invigorated. They still had most of the day ahead of them. Maybe, if she was lucky and the case broke the way she felt it might, she'd be back in Richmond by the close of the weekend to see Michelle one more time—if, that was, Melissa would allow it.

See, some wiser part of her spoke up as she got back behind the wheel of the car. *Even in the midst of multiple bloody murders, you're thinking of your granddaughter—of your family. Doesn't that tell you something?*

She supposed it did. But even as she stepped foot into the later quarter or so of her life, it was still very hard to admit that there was something more to life than her work. It was especially hard when she was on the trail of a killer and knew that at any moment, he could be killing again.

28

CHAPTER SIX

A small conference room in the back of the City of Roanoke Police had been set aside for Kate and DeMarco. Once they arrived at the station, a small portly woman at the front desk led them through the building and to the room. As soon as they sat down and started to set up a makeshift workstation, there was a knock at the door.

"Come in," Kate said.

When the door opened, they saw a familiar face—Palmetto from the State PD, the somewhat curmudgeonly man who had met them in front of the Nash residence much earlier in the day.

"I saw you guys headed back this way while I was signing all of my paperwork," Palmetto said. "I'm on the way out, driving back to Chesterfield in a few hours. I thought I'd check in to see if there was anything else I could help with."

"Nothing big," Kate said. "Did you happen to know that there was also a scrap of that same fabric discovered in the throat of Bethany Langley?"

"I didn't until about half an hour ago. Apparently, one of you called the lab to ask them to send a picture."

"Yeah," DeMarco said. "And it seems to be a match with the one you gave us."

At the mention of the scrap of fabric, Kate set the plastic bag Palmetto had given her on the table. "As of right now, it's the only solid evidence we have that links the murders in any concrete way."

"And forensics found pretty much nothing on that one," Palmetto said. "Aside from Mrs. Nash's DNA."

"The forensic report I'm seeing from the scrap from the Langleys offers up nothing, either," DeMarco said.

"Still might be worth a trip to the forensics lab," Kate said.

"Good luck with that," Palmetto said. "When I spoke with them about the Nash scrap, they were clueless."

"Were you at all involved with the scene at the Langley home?" Kate asked.

"No. I came in right after it had happened. I saw the bodies and checked the place over, but there was nothing. When you talk to forensics, though, ask them about the stray hair found on the clean laundry. It didn't seem to belong to Mrs. Langley, so they're going to run some tests on it."

"Before you go," Kate said, "do you want to offer up any theories?"

"I don't have one," Palmetto said dryly. "From the digging I've done, there seems to be absolutely *no* link between the Nashes and the Langleys. The fabric in the throats, though...something that personal and explicit to the killer *has* to link them somehow, right?"

"That's my thought," Kate said.

Palmetto gave the door a playful slap and then Kate saw him smile for the first time. "I'm sure you'll figure it out. I've heard about you, you know? A lot of us on the State PD have."

"I'm sure," she said with a smirk.

"Mostly good things. And then you came out of retirement to bring someone down a few months ago, right?"

"You could say that."

Palmetto, seeing that Kate wasn't going to just sit there and soak in accolades, gave her a shrug. "Give the state boys a call if you need anything on this one, Agent Wise."

"I'll do that," Kate said as Palmetto took his leave.

When Palmetto had closed the door behind him, DeMarco playfully shook her head. "You ever get tired of hearing people sing your praises?"

"Yes, actually," Kate said, but not in a rude way. While it was uplifting to be reminded of all that she had done throughout her career, she knew deep down that she had always just been doing her job. Perhaps she done her job with a bit more passion than others had, but it had been just that—a job well done...a job she could not seem to leave behind her.

Within a few minutes and some help from the station's systems administrator, Kate and DeMarco had access to the station's database. They worked together, looking into the pasts of the Nashes and the Langleys. Neither family had records of any kind. In fact, both families had records that made it hard to imagine anyone having a grudge against them. As for the Langleys, they had served as foster parents for a few years of their lives, so they'd had to undergo rigorous background checks several times throughout the course of their lives. The Nashes were heavily involved in their church and had been on several mission trips in the past twenty tears, most notably to Nepal and Honduras.

Kate gave up after a while and started pacing the floor. She used the conference room's dry erase board to jot down notes, hoping that seeing everything written down in one place would help her to focus. But there was nothing. No link, no clues, no clear course of where to go.

"You, too, huh?" DeMarco said. "Nothing?"

"Not so far. I think maybe we just go with what we *do* have rather than trying to find something new. I think we need to reevaluate the fabrics. While the forensics tests came up with nothing, maybe the fabric itself can point us somewhere."

"I don't follow you," DeMarco said.

"That's fine," Kate said. "I'm not sure I do, either. But I'm hoping we'll know it when we see it."

***

Kate felt the first true pangs of fatigue as she and DeMarco drove from the police station to the forensics lab. It was a stark reminder that she had not slept in about twenty-seven hours and that her work day had started insanely early. Twenty years ago, this would not have bothered her. But with fifty-six staring her right in the face from a few weeks across the calendar, things were different now.

The drive to the lab was only five minutes, located in close proximity to a little network consisting of the PD, the courthouse, and a holding jail. After showing their IDs, they were escorted past the front desk of the forensic sciences lab and into the central laboratory area. They were asked to sit in a small lobby for a moment while the technician who had been in charge of the fabric swabs was paged.

"You think there's any chance the fabric is just some kind of calling card for the killer?" DeMarco asked.

"It could be. Might not have anything to do with the *why* of the case. It could just mean something to the killer. Either way, right now it seems that the fabric—from a blanket of some kind, I feel quite sure—is our only real connection to him."

It made Kate recall a gruesome case she'd once been a part of early in the nineties. A man had killed five people—all ex-girlfriends. Before killing them by choking them, he had forced each one to swallow a condom. In the end, he had no real reason for doing so other than his hatred for wearing condoms during sex. Kate could not help but wonder if these fabric fragments would turn out to be just as insignificant to the case.

Their wait was a short one; a tall older man came hurrying out of a door directly across from them. "You're with the FBI?" he asked.

31

"We are," Kate said, showing her ID. DeMarco did the same and the man studied each one quite carefully.

"Nice to meet you, Agents," he said. "I'm Will Reed, and I ran the tests on the fabric from the recent murders. I assume that's why you're here? Agent DeMarco, I believe you are the one I sent the picture to earlier?"

"That's right," DeMarco said. "We were hoping you could shed some more light on those scraps."

"Well, I'd be more than happy to assist with whatever you need, but if it's about those two scraps of fabric, I'm afraid there's nothing I can offer. It seems that the killer not only went through great lengths to shove the fabric into the mouths of the victims, but that he was also quite careful about not leaving any traces of himself behind."

"Yes, we understand that," Kate said. "But without any firm physical results to go on, I was wondering if there's anything you could tell me about the fabric itself."

"Oh," Reed said. "That, I *can* help with."

"I'm of the opinion that both scraps came from the same source material," Kate said. "Most likely a blanket."

"I think that's a safe bet to place," Reed said. "I wasn't too sure until I saw the second scrap. They fit together rather well—color, texture, and so forth."

"Is there any way to tell how old the blanket might be?" Kate asked.

"I'm afraid not. What I can tell you, though, is what the blanket is made up of. And it stuck with me because as far as I know, it's an odd fabric combination for a traditional blanket as you'd think of one. The vast majority of the blanket is made of wool, which, of course, is not uncommon at all. But the secondary material used in the fabric is bamboo cotton."

"Is that all that different from *regular* cotton?" Kate asked.

"I'm not positive," he said. "But we see a lot of clothes and fabric-related material come through here. And I can count on one hand the number of times I've come into contact with something with noticeable traces of bamboo cotton. It's not a very rare material but it's just not as widespread as your basic cotton."

"In other words," DeMarco said, "it wouldn't be too hard to locate companies that use it as a primary material?"

"That, I *don't* know," Reed said. "But you may be interested to know that bamboo cotton *is* present in lots of fluffier blankets. It's quite breathable from what I've seen. You're probably looking for something on the pricier side. As a matter of fact, there's a warehouse just outside of town that manufactures the very sort of thing I mean. Pricy blankets, throws, sheets, that sort of thing."

"Do you know the name of it?" DeMarco asked.

"Biltmore Threads. They're a smaller company that nearly went belly up when everyone started buying everything online."

"Anything else you can tell us?" Kate asked.

"Yes, but it's sort of grisly. With the Nash woman, I believe the fabric was shoved so far down that she nearly vomited, even that close to death. There was stomach acid on the fabric."

Kate thought about the amount of force and effort it would take for someone to do that…about how much of one's hand would go into the victim's mouth.

"Thank you for your time, Mr. Reed," Kate said.

"Certainly. Let's just hope I don't see a third piece to that blanket anytime soon."

CHAPTER SEVEN

Eerily enough, the drive to the Biltmore Threads warehouse took Kate and DeMarco down the same stretch of road they had taken into Whip Springs at four o'clock that morning. The factory and warehouse were located down a two-lane road that snaked off of the main highway. It was tucked away, along with the stretch of dying grass that served as its landscaping, in the very same woods that had hidden the Nash home from the main road.

From the looks of the parking lot, Biltmore Threads wasn't doing quite as badly as Will Reed had suggested. The place looked to employ at least fifty or so people, and that was based on just this time of day. With a factory like this, Kate assumed there was shift work involved, meaning another fifty or so would probably come in later on for the night shift.

They made their way inside, walking into a dingy lobby. A woman sitting behind a counter looked up at them with a peculiar expression. It was evident that they didn't get many visitors.

"Can I help you?" she asked.

DeMarco went through the round of introductions and after they showed their IDs, the woman at the counter buzzed them in through a door on the far end of the lobby. That same woman met them there and then led them down a small hallway. At the end of the hall, she opened a set of double doors that led onto the Biltmore Threads production floor. Several sets of looms and other equipment Kate had never seen were thrumming with life. On the far side of the large work floor, a compact forklift was carrying a pallet of stacked cloth elsewhere into the warehouse.

After leading them carefully around the edge of the floor, the woman stopped at another door and led them inside. Here, there was a thin hallway adorned with five rooms. The woman brought them to the first one and knocked.

"Yeah?" a man's voice boomed from inside.

"We've got visitors," the woman called before opening the door. "Two ladies from the FBI."

There was a few seconds' pause and then the door was opened from the other side. A dark-haired man wearing thick glasses greeted them. He looked them up and down, not out of nervousness but sheer curiosity.

34

"FBI?" he asked. "What can I do for you?"

"Can we have a minute of your time?" Kate asked.

"Sure," he said, standing aside and allowing them into his office.

There was only one seat in the office other than the one behind his desk. Neither Kate nor DeMarco took it. The dark-haired man did not take his seat either, electing to stand with them.

"I assume you're the supervisor?" Kate asked.

"I'm the regional manager and day shift supervisor, yes," he said. He extended his hand quickly, as if embarrassed he had forgotten to so earlier than this. "Ray Garraty."

Kate shook the offered hand and then showed her ID. She then reached into her pocket and withdrew the scrap of fabric from the Nash scene.

"This is a scrap of fabric from a recent crime scene," she said. "And we believe it could be key in catching a killer. The forensics lab found bamboo cotton in it, and I understand that Biltmore Threads uses bamboo cotton rather regularly."

"We do," Garraty said. He reached for the bag and then hesitated before asking: "Do you mind?"

Kate shook her head and handed it to him. Garraty looked it over closely and nodded. "Without actually tearing it further apart, I can't give you any guarantees, but yeah, it looks to have some in it. Do you know where the fabric came from?"

"I'm assuming a blanket," Kate said.

"Looks like it," Garraty said. "And while I'm not one hundred percent sure, I think it might have been designed and manufactured here."

"Right here at Biltmore Threads?" Kate asked.

"Perhaps."

Garraty handed the plastic bag back to Kate and then walked to an old beaten-up filing cabinet tucked away in the back corner of the small office. He opened the bottom drawer and after fishing through its contents for a while, pulled out two different books. They were both quite large and as he started leafing through one, Kate saw that they were both inventory catalogues.

"The color and the design you can sort of make out look familiar," Garraty explained as he went through the pages. "If it was made here, it will be in one of these books."

It was an exciting thought, but Kate wasn't quite sure what it would mean. If the blanket in question *was* made in Biltmore Threads, did it really even open up that many possibilities? There were many more questions to ask before coming to such a conclusion.

"Right here," Garraty said. He turned the book toward them and pointed to one of several different blankets listed on a page about three-quarters of the way through one of the books. "Does that look like a match to you?"

Kate and DeMarco both studied the page. Kate looked back and forth, making sure she wasn't *making* herself see some semblance of similarity. But after a few seconds, DeMarco answered for her.

"I mean, the fabric we have is faded, but it's the same. Even that little faded white checkered pattern."

"Well, it's faded because it's an older product," Garraty said. He pointed to a line from the item description. "Right here, it says it started being produced in 1991 and was eliminated from our production cycle in 2004."

"So you made this same blanket for thirteen years?" DeMarco asked.

"Yes. It was a very popular item, which is how I was able to recognize it so quickly."

"In other words, the last time you would have passed this blanket out of your warehouse was 2004," Kate said. "Meaning that this sample is somewhere between fifteen and thirty years old."

"That's correct."

Well, even if there could *be a link due to the blanket,* Kate thought, *that thirty-year window makes it* very *hard.*

"Mr. Garraty, how long have you been in your position here?"

"Going on twenty-six years," Garraty said. "I've got retirement coming up next year."

"While you've been here, has Biltmore Threads employed Scott or Bethany Langley, or Toni or Derrick Nash?"

Garraty thought about it for a moment and then shrugged. "The names don't ring any bells for me, but if we're looking over a span of more than ten years, I'd refer you to records. There are a lot of employees that come in and out of here."

"How soon can you find out for sure?" DeMarco asked.

"Within the hour."

"That would be appreciated," Kate said. "And if you don't mind, just one more question. Have you had any employees cause problems for you or the factory in the past month or so? Any troublemakers or just someone you and other management knew to keep an eye on?"

"Funny you should ask," Garraty said. "I had to fire a guy just two weeks ago. He was showing up to work stoned *and* we were pretty sure he was stealing material. When I confronted him about it, he got violent and I had to call security. And since we only have one security guard, the police got involved and he was eventually arrested. But he was out the next day."

"Stealing material?" DeMarco said, an edge of excitement to her voice.

"Yes…but not that one," he said, pointing to the plastic bag. "If that's been discontinued, we haven't had that fabric in the warehouse for *years*. No, he came out and told us later, when he cooled down, that he had been stealing it for some projects his girlfriend was creating. She has an Etsy shop or something."

"Can we get a name?" Kate asked.

"Travis Rogers. He's about thirty years old. Has a record, I think. Some mild violent crimes. But we tend to give people a second chance at Biltmore Threads, you know?"

"Is he a local?" DeMarco asked.

"Yeah, over in Whip Springs. I can get you his address."

"Again, that would be appreciated," Kate said.

Garraty led them out of his office and back down the same path the receptionist had led them, only in reverse. When they were back in the lobby, Garraty spoke with the receptionist while Kate and DeMarco huddled by the lobby doors.

"The blanket being manufactured here," DeMarco said. "You think that's just a creepy coincidence?"

"It could be. I'm inclined to think so, given that the blanket hasn't been produced in so long. It *does* make me wonder, though…"

"Wonder what?"

"No matter where the blanket was from, we know that it's got to be old…at least fifteen years and as much as about thirty. And if that's the case, it makes me think someone held on to it. Why use something so old unless it has some sort of meaning or significance to you?"

She let the question linger as Garraty walked back over to them. He handed Kate a slip of paper with an address scrawled on it.

"I also went ahead and had her look to see if any of those names you gave me were in the system as former employees," Garraty said. "We got nothing."

"That's fine," Kate said. "It just needed to be checked. Thank you for your help."

"Glad to do it," Garraty said, still looking as if the entire visit had thrown him off.

Kate and DeMarco headed back outside. As they headed for the car, Kate looked past the dead lawn in front of the factory and warehouse. The expanse of trees made her nervous in a way she could not explain. Thick forests had always made her feel like that; they offered far too many places to hide. She gave the woods a skeptical look as she got back behind the wheel.

"GPS says this Travis Rogers lives less than half an hour away, on the other side of Roanoke."

"Then let's pay him a visit," Kate said.

Maybe it was because the day had started so early or maybe it was because she could feel herself getting more and more tired by the minute, but she was starting to get a good feeling about this case—a feeling that it might be over much sooner rather than later.

She pulled out of the parking lot of Biltmore Threads desperately hoping that she was right.

CHAPTER EIGHT

Travis Rogers lived in a townhouse not too far away from the thick traffic of a mall complex. Given that it was creeping up on lunchtime, the traffic was pretty bad as Kate neared the place. Passing a Starbucks and a Dunkin' Donuts also made her realize that, unprofessional or not, she was going to have to stop for coffee after they questioned Travis Rogers or she might very well fall asleep on the job.

She soldiered through and parked in front of the townhouse about forty minutes after leaving Biltmore Threads. She and DeMarco hustled up to the front door, neither of them having much hope that a man in his thirties would be at home in the middle of the day—especially not one who would likely be searching for a job.

So they were both surprised when the door was answered by a ruggedly handsome man. He looked a little scraggly around the edges but well-groomed. He *did* look a little tired, though, maybe like he had just rolled out of bed.

"Are you Travis Rogers?" DeMarco asked.

"I am. Who's asking?"

DeMarco took the lead this time, showing her badge and taking a step toward the door to let him know that they weren't going to be turned away.

"FBI? What the hell for?"

"Your name came up in passing in regards to a case we're working," Kate asked. "If you'd give us just five minutes of your time, we can be on our way."

Clearly confused and a little alarmed, Travis stepped to the side and opened the door. When he did, Kate saw that his right hand was in a cast from high on the wrist, all the way to the knuckles of his fingers.

It'd be pretty hard to kill someone the way the Nashes and Langleys were killed if you had a cast on your right hand, Kate told herself.

The front door opened into the living room, which was quite clean. A laptop sat on the coffee table. She saw a LinkedIn profile on the screen; apparently Travis was indeed doing some job hunting.

"I'm going to assume this is about what happened with the whole thing at Biltmore Threads, right?" Travis said as he sat down on the couch. "Although I don't know why the FBI would get involved in something that small."

"Can I ask why you got violent with Mr. Garraty?" Kate asked.

"It was just months and months of frustration, you know? I'd been asking for a raise for about half a year. I'd been there for almost five years and had only gotten two small pay bumps, so I thought I was due. Garraty basically told me that he could pass on my complaint but if I kept pestering them, it was going to look bad. We had some words and, quite frankly, I lost my shit. I threw his little name placard thing from his desk at him. I started to rush across the room at him but thought better of it."

"And what about your past offenses?"

"A bar fight when I was nineteen and then defending myself when some dipshit lost his cool in a fit of road rage when I accidentally clipped his car. Not to be a smart ass, but you're welcome to look all of that up. Look…this whole thing with Garraty and Biltmore Threads…it's embarrassing. So if there's anything you need from me, just let me know. I'd like to get it behind me as soon as I can."

"Well, what about the material you were stealing?" DeMarco asked.

"I only did it twice, and that was *after* I had started to get pissed off about not being paid fairly. I'm not proud of it. But I've been to court and I'm going to pay the fines."

"Garraty said you stole the materials for your girlfriend."

"Yeah. Jess runs this little Etsy shop. She makes these trendy little custom clutch purses and shoulder bags. She makes more than I did doing it…so yeah, I took some material for her."

Kate was all but certain that Travis was innocent. He'd made some dumb choices, sure, and he had unfortunate luck when it came to physical altercations, but he sure as hell wasn't a murderer.

"What happened to your hand?" DeMarco asked.

Travis rolled his eyes and looked at the floor. "Just another genius decision on my part. I was so pissed when the cops got called on me at Biltmore Threads that I punched the wall outside the building. It's a brick wall, and it hurt like a bitch. I broke three fingers and got a hairline fracture down the base of my hand."

"Do you have any proof of when you did this?" DeMarco asked.

"Yeah. Actually, the first bill for the x-ray came today." He got up and went to the edge of the counter in the attached kitchen. He

40

retrieved a piece of mail from it and brought it back to them. Kate and DeMarco looked it over and saw that the initial consult for the x-ray had been three weeks ago—at least two full weeks before the Langleys had been murdered.

"At the risk of sounding nosy, can I ask what this is about?" Travis asked.

Kate had just one more thing left to do. She almost decided against it because she was *that* certain that Travis Rogers was innocent. She took the evidence bag with the scrap of blanket inside of it and showed it to him.

"Does this look familiar to you?" she asked.

His initial reaction told her what she needed to know. There was no alarm, no guilt, no fear. He merely looked closely at it and shrugged. "I don't think so. Is it something from Biltmore Threads?"

"It is," Kate said, pocketing the bag again. "Thank you for your time, Mr. Rogers."

When they headed back out to the car, the feeling Kate had experienced coming out of Biltmore Threads started to unravel. The blanket fabric coming from Biltmore had seem like an omen of sorts, a sign that they were on the right track. But now, back to having no leads whatsoever, she felt a little lost.

"You think we should try speaking to the neighbors of the victims now?" DeMarco asked when they were back in the car.

"That's the best idea I can think of," Kate said. "Of course, the Nashes had no immediate neighbors—no one who would be able to see any coming and going from around their house."

"So the Langleys, then," DeMarco said.

"Right," Kate agreed. "But first...I have to get some coffee. This whole regular-sleep thing that comes with retirement has ruined me."

***

Coffee in hand, Kate stepped out of the car adjacent to the Langley residence. She looked to the house next to it and realized that they may have hit the jackpot. While she hated to give in to stereotypes—especially in her line of work—there was one that she had found *usually* proved itself true: the older the woman, the more prone they were to gossip. And there was just such a woman standing on the porch next door to the Langley home. She was carefully filling a bird feeder with some sort of liquid. A hummingbird feeder, if Kate was seeing it correctly.

41

Kate and DeMarco approached slowly, not wanting to seem threatening or in a hurry. The woman gave them an uncertain smile as she finished up with the bird feeder. It swung gently as she released it, the red liquid she had just put inside of it looking almost like Kool-Aid.

"Hummingbirds?" Kate asked.

"That's right," the old woman said. She was pushing seventy…maybe eighty. It was hard to tell due to the beaming smile on her face. "They come by and see me at least twice a day as long as I keep the feeder full. Now…can I help you ladies?"

"Yes, ma'am. I'm Agent Wise, and this is Agent DeMarco," Kate said, showing her ID. "We've been assigned to the case involving the Langleys and were hoping you could take some time to speak with us."

The woman looked over Kate's shoulder, toward the Langley house. The radiant smile on her face was gone now. There was no frown there, either…just a resigned look. A *what-has-the-world-come-to* look.

"Nice to meet you agents, I suppose," the woman said. She hunkered down in a lawn chair that sat against the porch rails and looked up at them. "I'm Callie Spencer, by the way. Been living here in this house for about twenty-five years now."

"So you've been here the entire time the Langleys lived there?"

"Yes indeed. Scott and Bethany moved in sometime in the early nineties, I'd say."

"Would you call them friendly?" DeMarco asked. "Social?"

"I guess so. I mean, they weren't rude or mean or anything like that. They were an okay couple, but a little private. Especially over the last few years."

"Any idea why?" Kate asked.

Callie frowned and nodded. "Bethany sort of got different after her sister died in that car accident. Ten years ago or so, I suppose."

"Can you expand on what you mean by *private*?" DeMarco asked.

"Well, you know…*private* might not be the best word. If we crossed paths on the sidewalk, we'd chat it up for a while. But they never came over just to visit. Never really volunteered any information. Scott would catch me out trying to mow the lawn from time to time and insist on finishing. So, no, not private but not really outgoing, either."

"Do you know if they had any regular visitors?" Kate asked.

"None that I know of. I believe Scott had a friend or two from work come over every now and then during football season. And there was a period of time, you know, when Davey was living with them."

"Davey?" Kate asked.

"Yes. Well, I called him Davey. His real name is David. He's their nephew—the son of Bethany's sister. When she died, he came and stayed with them. He was only ten years old. He'd stay with the Langleys for a while and then would go away for months at a time. I found out later from Scott that during those times, he was staying with his uncle from his father's side down in Texas."

Kate and DeMarco shared a look. This wasn't necessarily a lead, but it was new information that could take them several different places. "Do you happen to know how long ago Davey was still living with them?"

"Oh, I think he moved out for good two or three years ago. About time, too. I felt sorry for him, you know? Passed back and forth between families. But the Langleys were good for him, I think. They were sweet people. They were foster parents. Did you know that?"

"Yes ma'am," Kate said, recalling the information they had found while digging around at the Roanoke Police Department.

"When was the last time they fostered someone?" DeMarco asked.

"Oh, I can't say with any certainty. At least a few years, I think. One time they kept this little girl for a few months. The sweetest thing. She'd come over here and we'd play checkers on the porch."

"And what about Davey?" Kate asked. "Did you have many interactions with him?"

"Not many. They were keeping Davey for the first go-round when my husband passed away. They all came over here—Davey, too—and gave their condolences. But, you know, being neighbors, it's pretty easy to sort of just *see* things about people, you know? And with Davey, he was always very quiet. He had this sort of brooding quality to him. I do know that as he got older, he became very hard to handle. Defiant, I guess."

"Do you know where he ended up after leaving the Langleys' care?" DeMarco asked.

"Oh, he's still around. He ended up going to community college but he ended up dropping out. I don't know why...grades, or just no commitment, maybe. I'm not sure where he's living but I *do* know where he works. He's been working at Gino's Pizza for at least several months now."

"You're certain of this?" Kate asked.

"I know he was working there oh, about six months ago, because he delivered a pizza to my door. I usually think it's stupid to have pizza delivered because then you have to give a tip, but I was sick, so…" She realized she was trailing off here. She smiled, rolled her eyes at herself, and continued. "Anyway, and then my friend Janell, whom I have tea with twice a week, said she saw him working down at Gino's not too long ago. Maybe about two or three weeks."

"Thank you," Kate said.

"Hold on, wait. You don't think Davey had anything to do with their murders, do you?"

"Most likely not," Kate said. "But he'd be a great source of information about the family. And right now, every bit of information is critical."

Callie seemed relieved at this, giving them a nod. As she did, a hummingbird floated into view at the feeder. The three women watched it for a moment, the smile returning to Callie's face.

"I do hope you can find who did this," Callie said. "Rumor has it that a family out in Whip Springs was killed, too. A husband and wife. Is that right?"

"We can't comment on that," Kate said, hating the sound of it. She knew that to someone like Callie Spencer, that noncommittal comment would sound like a big fat *yes*.

"Well, best of luck, Agents," Callie said as Kate and DeMarco started back down the stairs.

DeMarco got behind the wheel this time. As Kate opened the passenger door, she looked back to Callie Spencer on her porch. She was staring hard at the hummingbird—which had now been joined by two more. It was then that Kate realized that Callie wasn't so much interested in the birds, as she was intent on not looking in the direction of the Langleys' house. Finding something both sad and comforting about this, Kate got into the car and pulled up directions for Gino's Pizza.

CHAPTER NINE

They arrived at Gino's just as the lunch rush had apparently died down. Once inside, Kate's stomach responded right away to the delicious smell of pizza and calzones. She could barely remember grabbing breakfast that morning seeing as how much of the earlier part of the day seemed to be nothing more than a blur.

"Hungry?" DeMarco asked.

"You read my mind."

They approached the small booth adorned with a sign reading Please Wait to Be Seated. A teenaged girl greeted them with a smile. "Table for two?" she asked.

"And, if you don't mind, we'd like to speak to a young man that works here. Is Davey here today?"

"No, not today," the hostess said.

"How about the manager?" DeMarco asked. "Is he here?"

"Yes. Do you need to speak with him?"

"Yes, please," Kate said. She looked around the place and saw that it was practically dead. She wondered if this was a reflection of the food but her stomach was too hungry to really care. So she added: "While we eat, if you don't mind."

The hostess led them to a table at the back of the restaurant, took their drink orders, and headed back toward the kitchen area. After looking over the menu and deciding that they were both starving, Kate and DeMarco opted for a large pizza. They bickered over toppings for a moment—DeMarco was one of the oddballs who thought pineapple belonged on pizza—and it brought a smile to Kate's face. This was only the second case they had worked together and they had a natural chemistry that most partners took a long time to build.

I really need to get to know her better, Kate thought.

The hostess came back three minutes later with their drinks. A hefty middle-aged man was with her. His little nameplate pinned to the breast of his shirt read *Teddy.* The hostess took their order, leaving them with Teddy. He looked at both of them with a nervous look on his face, perhaps assuming they wanted to complain about the service or the employee they had mentioned by name to the hostess.

"I'm Teddy King," the man said in a soothing tone. It was the sort of tone someone who was used to making apologies tended to adapt to. "I was told you needed to speak with the manager?"

"Yes," Kate said. She again took a look around the place. If there had been more patrons (there were currently only three, all older people sitting together on the opposite side of the restaurant), she would not be speaking about the case at a table, out in the open. But this place was currently about as private and quiet as anyplace else. She took out her ID and plopped it on the table, not wanting to give those other three patrons the opportunity to see it if they happened to look over in this direction.

"I'm Agent Wise with the FBI, and this is my partner, Agent DeMarco. We're working a case that has led us to one of your employees, a young man named Davey."

"That would be Davey Armstrong," Teddy said. Kate thought she caught an edge of irritation in his voice.

"It sounds like you aren't too surprised that the authorities might be looking for him," Kate pointed out.

Teddy sat down at the chair at the edge of the table and shrugged. "Well, I mean I wouldn't paint him as a criminal or anything, but he's just the sort that always makes you feel on edge. He's a decent employee when he wants to be, I guess. A little lazy at times. I've nearly fired him on two different occasions, but…I don't know. I'm a sucker for a sob story."

"What's the version of his sob story that you've heard?" Kate asked.

"Well, I knew his mother. Went to high school with her. And when he came in looking for a job about a year or so ago, I made the connection right away. I'd sort of kept up with him through word of mouth after his mom died. He was bounced around from family member to family member, never really having a home. I talked to him one time about his mother, just to let him know I had known her and thought she was an amazing woman. It made him sad but he seemed to enjoy hearing it. But even then, when trying to connect with him, I felt like it might have been a mistake to hire him."

"A mistake?" DeMarco asked. "Why is that?"

"Well, he's just not very responsible. He's twenty-six and just isn't motivated. And he's not very good with people. After I realized this, I made a point to put him on as a delivery driver— keeping him out of the shop and away from paying customers, you know? Plus, he just sometimes gets this look about him that— forgive me for saying so—creeps people right the hell out. I've had waitresses complain about it. And you know, he seems to prefer that…being out in the car, driving around and delivering food."

"If I were to give you a few small windows of time, would you be able to tell me if Davey was making deliveries during those times?"

"Yeah. Just let me go grab the schedule."

Teddy got up, leaving Kate and DeMarco to mull over what they had just heard. Kate tried to imagine a lackluster twenty-six-year-old who had been dealt a rough hand at life working in a place like this. Even driving deliveries around, she supposed she could see how someone like Davey Armstrong might seem to have a storm cloud on his heels at all times.

Teddy came back with the schedule and sat back down. He also brought their pizza with him. Kate was impressed. It had taken less than ten minutes to get it—which, in her experience, had to be a record of some kind. Maybe it was the FBI badge and ID. It came with certain perks, and apparently getting pizza quickly was one of them.

"The first date would be yesterday, sometime between lunch and six in the afternoon," Kate said. "The other isn't as certain, but would likely have been four or five days ago. So let's say Monday or Tuesday."

Teddy scanned the schedule and pointed to a column with Davey's name at the top. "Well, he was off Monday, but he worked the seven-hour stretch from two-to-nine on Tuesday night. And then yes, he was working yesterday from five in the afternoon until closing."

"Did you happen to notice anything off about him on either of those days?" Kate asked.

"Well, like I said…he always seemed a little off. But no…I didn't notice anything out of the ordinary. Although…"

He stopped here, as if a thought had just sprung to the forefront of his mind.

"What is it?" Kate asked.

"He was late as hell getting back from one of those deliveries on Tuesday. I didn't lay into him too badly because we weren't all that busy. He claimed he knocked and knocked on this person's door but it took them forever to show up. Said that was why he was late."

"How late are we talking?" DeMarco asked.

"The run there and back should have only taken him about half an hour but he was gone for a little over an hour."

"Can we get the addresses he delivered to during that run?"

"Sure. I'll have to look back through the receipts and orders, though. Might take a few minutes."

"No hurry," Kate said. "When you do get the information, just give us a call." She slid a business card over to him and then added: "By any chance did you ever happen to hear him talk ill about the Langley family?"

"Not at all. He liked them quite a bit. Why…is there something wrong?"

Kate did not want to tell this man the news of the Langleys. She was actually surprised he had not yet heard it. It made Kate wonder if Davey had learned of the fate of the family that had raised him for a while.

"I'm afraid Scott and Bethany were killed three days ago."

"Oh my God," Teddy said. "Well, I don't think Davey has any idea. Three days ago?"

"It appears that way," DeMarco said.

"And you think Davey had something to do with it?"

"It's far too early to make such a speculation," Kate said. "Do you happen to know where he lives?"

"I do, actually. I had to give him a few rides home when his car was on the mend. And I'm pretty sure you'd catch him there right now. He might not seem very committed to work, but he's sure as hell committed to Fortnite."

Kate had heard of Fortnite; she was pretty sure it was a recent online game that was insanely popular with teens. She didn't want to say anything, though, because she wasn't quite sure.

Ah, old age strikes again, she thought.

"Would you mind giving us the address?" Kate asked.

"I don't know the exact address, but I can give you the directions. You won't be able to miss it. He listens to his music so damned loud that his neighbors have called in noise complaints on him."

"That would be fine," Kate said.

And as Teddy gave them directions to Davey's apartment, Kate's mind wandered a bit. How could Davey not know about the deaths of the people who had helped raise him? It seemed peculiar to her. But even more peculiar than that was the idea that maybe he *did* know and had decided to keep it to himself, deciding not to tell Teddy or anyone he worked with.

And why would he do that? Kate could only think of one thing: because he was hiding a degree of guilt.

CHAPTER TEN

A simple call to the police was enough for Kate to discover that Davey Armstrong had *not* been informed of the Langleys' deaths. He was not listed as next of kin in any reports, the only link being a doctor's form from eight years ago where Bethany Langley had been listed as his emergency contact.

This made the impromptu visit all the more pivotal. Not only were they going to be questioning him about his whereabouts during the time of the murders and get a gauge on his mental state, but they were apparently going to be informing him of the deaths of his aunt and uncle.

Teddy's directions had been quite detailed, so they found the apartment complex with no problem. It was actually not so much a complex as it was a large house-looking structure with five separate living quarters. It was in a small complex with three other structures. As Kate and DeMarco got out of the car, they heard yet another of Teddy's details that turned out to be spot on: the booming sound of music turned up to an obnoxious volume. It was some sort of heavy metal from what Kate could tell, grinding guitars and a machine-gun-fire beat from double bass drums.

It was coming from apartment 3B, just as Teddy had said. The agents approached the door and Kate wasted no time trying to be polite. She pounded hard on the door, making sure she could be heard over the roar of the music. A demonic, throaty voice had joined in with the guitars and drums now.

After a few moments, the music came to a stop. Hurried footsteps could be heard coming toward the door. It opened quickly, but only enough for a hectic-looking man to peer through the doorway at them.

"Yeah?" he asked, clearly feeling that he was being horribly inconvenienced.

"Are you David Armstrong?" Kate asked.

"Yeah. And you are?"

Kate and DeMarco showed their IDs almost in perfect sync. Davey studied them with great interest, his expression going from awe to fright. He looked suspiciously at them but still showed an edge of irritation.

"I'm Agent Wise, and this is my partner Agent DeMarco. It has come to our attention that you are the nephew of Scott and Bethany Langley."

"I am," he said. He then peeked over his shoulder. Kate could see a computer behind him, the screen on some game menu screen. "Why is the FBI interested in me *or* the Langleys?"

"Can we come in?" Kate asked.

"Is that really necessary?" Davey asked.

"It would make things much easier and we'd be out of your hair faster," Kate said.

"Fine."

Davey stepped to the side and allowed them inside. As they passed through the doorway, DeMarco wasted little time. "When was the last time you spoke with them?" she asked.

"I don't know," Davey said. He sat down behind his computer desk and checked something on the screen. Kate assumed he was playing Fortnite, as Teddy had suggested. "Maybe a month or so. Aunt Bethany called to say hi. Just sort of checking in."

Kate looked to DeMarco and gave her a look that she hoped communicated to *"Don't worry, I've got this."*

"Mr. Armstrong, I'm sorry to be the one to tell you this, but Bethany and Scott are dead. They were killed in their home four or five days ago."

Something similar to shock washed over Davey's face but it didn't stay there for very long. He looked at the floor for a moment and it was then that Kate was certain he would break into tears. But he did nothing of the sort. He looked back up at the agents, looking back and forth between the two of them.

"Do you know who did it yet?" Davey asked. "Have you caught them?"

"No," DeMarco said. "That's why we're here. We were hoping you might be able to shed some light on why someone might want to kill them."

"Oh," he said, rather absently. He at least seemed to not care as much about the game behind him, but he also didn't seem quite as upset as Kate had expected. He looked detached—almost as if he was thinking about something else entirely. "Yeah, I don't know. They were good, you know? Good people. I can't think of anyone that would want to kill them…"

"Davey, are you okay?" Kate asked.

He looked up at her then and when he did, she saw the fear in his eyes. He was scared and clearly uneasy. Kate knew that the human mind went through a ton of stages as it tried to accept monumental loss, but this seemed out of place.

"And you're certain you hadn't spoken to them recently?" Kate asked.

"I told you, it's been weeks," he said, snapping at her. "Look…I just need to go. I need to get out of here and…"

He got up and headed for the door. He moved in such a way that for a split second, Kate thought he was going to attack— perhaps pulling a gun out. But he only made a beeline for the front door, doing everything he could not to look at them.

DeMarco surprised Kate by jumping to her feet and moving with catlike guile. She made it to the door before Davey, blocking his way.

"Davey, we know this is some miserable news to digest, but we really need you to stay here with us for a bit longer. Just a few more questions and we can—"

Davey let out a gut-churning scream that was half anger and half desperation. He threw a hard shoulder into DeMarco, sending her back hard against the doorframe. Just as her head rebounded from the frame, Davey bounded through the door. Kate noted that he had not fully closed it when they entered, indicating that he had planned to make a run for it from the start.

Kate leaped to her feet and chased after him. DeMarco looked a little woozy, bracing herself against the wall to make sure she didn't fall down. She took two huge strides after him as he slammed the door in her face from the outside. She blocked it with her forearm and pushed through it. She stepped out onto the porch just as Davey made it down the small flight of stairs.

Kate knew right away that she would not be able to match him in a footrace so she decided to take a chance to eliminate the race altogether. Rather than running after him, she took one big stride to the edge of the porch and launched herself forward. She knew right away that she had overestimated the distance; rather than take him in the back of the knees, she was going to end up slamming into his upper back.

She braced for the impact and felt a twinge of pain in her neck as they collided. Her full weight slammed into him from behind. He went down so quickly and so fast that as he fell, his legs nearly came up over his head in a half-flip. Kate managed to lock her right arm around his neck as they both fell, applying a rear-neck choke as they hit the ground, The air went out of her and the jarring pain that shot through her reminded her that she was well north of fifty years of age.

Still, the adrenaline was enough to help her roll on top of him, plant a knee in his back, and pull his arms behind him. She cuffed him with expert precision and was relieved when she heard DeMarco approaching from behind. With her help, they pulled Davey Armstrong to his feet. Kate hid a grimace when she saw that he had skinned up the side of his face in the fall. The fault was hers, though, as she could have been a bit gentler.

"Why'd you run?" DeMarco asked.

Davey said nothing. As they led him to the car, Kate hurried ahead. She popped open the trunk, hoping for a first-aid kit. She found one, plucked out the antibacterial wipes, and opened them. Before putting Davey in the back of the car, she wiped the blood away from the nasty scratch on his face. He winced at the sting but said nothing.

"Do you know why we're taking you with us, David?" DeMarco asked.

"Because they're dead," he said. "And I guess you think I did it."

As he scooted into the back seat, Kate and DeMarco shared an uneasy look over the roof of the car. "You okay?" DeMarco asked quietly.

Kate nodded, though it was hard to tell if she was hurt in any way. The adrenaline was still rushing through her. In that moment, she felt more than okay. She felt *great.*

"How about you?" Kate asked. "My head hurts. He gave me a good whack. But I'm okay."

"I should drive, then," Kate said.

"I'll call ahead to the station and let them know we're coming with a…with a what? I guess he's a suspect?"

"Seems that way," Kate said as she got behind the wheel.

She recalled the fear she had seen in his eyes and the absolute berserker speed and fury in his escape and scream. It made no sense to her that he would be the killer but then again, why was he remaining silent? Why did he run?

With the last dregs of adrenaline coursing through her, Kate pondered these questions. In the back of the car, Davey Armstrong remained quiet, as if sitting on some dark secret.

CHAPTER ELEVEN

Kate was nursing another cup of coffee and waiting for her turn to speak with Davey Armstrong. She was sitting with DeMarco in the conference room that was serving as their temporary office, watching footage on a mounted television on the wall as the police chief sat down across the table from Davey in an adjacent holding cell. There was no formal interrogation room in the City of Roanoke Police Department, so Davey was currently in an informal holding cell.

From what Kate could tell, Davey was still not talking. She stared at his silent figure on the screen, trying to work it out in her head.

"You think it fits?" DeMarco asked.

"He has the history to suggest that there might be some sort of strain between him and the Langleys, but no. Those murders were grisly. If he killed them, I think he'd be more interested in talking. Letting us know why. Letting us know *how*."

"What if he's just staying quiet because he wants to see how much more we know?" DeMarco asked. "What if he's killed more people and wants to know if we've discovered the bodies yet? The Nashes, for instance."

It was a good thought and one worth running with. On the screen, the chief started to get to his feet, apparently tired of trying to get Davey to talk. As he started heading for the door and partially off of the screen, Kate's cell phone rang. It was an unfamiliar number, with a Roanoke area code.

"Hello?" she said.

There was a man's voice on the other end. He spoke to her for about thirty seconds before Kate said, "Okay. Thank you so much."

She ended the call and started for the conference room door right away. "Come on," she told DeMarco. "We got him. Davey Armstrong is our killer after all."

***

Kate sat across from Davey, on the same chair the Chief of Police had sat in moments ago. She looked at Davey through the bars of the holding cell. DeMarco sat beside her, deep in thought about the revelation that Kate had just told her.

"I'm going to give you one last chance to say something," Kate said. "I just got a phone call that doesn't tell the entire story, but it tells *enough* of the story. Enough to formally arrest you for murder. So you have five seconds to figure out something to say."

Kate gave him the five seconds. She noticed DeMarco silently keeping count on her fingers as the seconds passed.

"Fine," Kate said. "Earlier today, we spoke with Teddy King, your manager at Gino's. He told us that on Tuesday afternoon, you were very late coming back from one of your deliveries. He just called me a few moments ago with the names and addresses you visited on that run. One of them was the home of Scott and Bethany Langley. And that just happens to be within the window of time in which they were killed. So...*now* do you have anything to say?"

He looked up at them with all the integrity of a trapped animal. He'd been caught and he knew it. He gave a lazy shrug and, for the first time since being told that his aunt and uncle had died, shed a tear.

"I lied before. I actually hadn't spoken to them in months," he said. "Maybe as much as a year. They weren't exactly happy with me. They didn't kick me out of their house, but strongly urged me to leave. So I enrolled in college, got a job and a place of my own. They'd try to stay in touch but I sort of froze them out."

"Why did they ask you to leave?" DeMarco asked.

"This was almost ten years ago," Davey said. "I'd started doing drugs. Just a little coke here and there. I wasn't an addict. Not then..."

He trailed off here, sensing that he was either getting off the point or not ready to face a truth that was trying to surface.

"Was there an altercation of some kind when you stopped to deliver their pizzas?" Kate asked.

"No. I didn't even knock on the door. I left the pizzas on the porch, beeped the horn on the car, and took off."

Kate didn't believe him. Not one bit. He was talking too fast, like someone saying the first thing that popped into their heads.

"When you deliver pizzas, do they have to sign anything?" Kate asked.

"No. Not unless they pay with a check."

She could see the uncertainty in his eyes as he tried to calculate his next move. She could practically see the wheels turning in his head as he tried to anticipate every way out of this conversation—

how to not get caught in a lie, how to answer each question in a way that wouldn't nail him down.

"How did the Langleys pay?" DeMarco asked. "If you just ditched the pizzas and ran, they had to have paid in advance, right?"

"Yeah. I guess they did. With Gino's, you can order online. We just started it a few months back. I guess they paid like that because the order didn't say anything about having to collect payment."

Kate considered all of this and made the decision to let it rest for now. Whether Davey realized it or not, he had just given them more than enough information. Based on everything he had just said, there would be *more* than enough to either catch him in a blatant lie or free him.

As for Kate, she was fully expecting a lie.

"Thanks, Mr. Armstrong," she said. "We do need to check on a few things but if you're telling the truth, you should be able to leave within a few hours."

"Check what?" he asked. "How the hell am I a suspect here?"

Kate smirked, unable to hide it. "Because I've been doing this long enough to know when I'm being lied to."

And with that, she left the room. She had expected Davey to voice some final truth as she left but he stayed silent. After a few seconds, DeMarco followed behind her, leaving Davey alone in the holding cell.

***

"Did you see his forearms?"

DeMarco asked the question almost half-heartedly. She was looking directly at the wall, as if looking at a diagram that had all of the answers to the case.

"No," Kate said. "Should I have looked at them?"

DeMarco shrugged. "I almost missed it. But there were track marks. Faint, but there. If I didn't have some history with it—a relative, not me, so don't worry—I wouldn't have even seen it."

"Heroin?" Kate asked.

"Yeah, pretty sure," DeMarco said.

"So maybe he's in denial about it?" Kate suggested. "Maybe he was late from those deliveries because he was using. Maybe the thought of having to see the Langleys stressed him out."

"Could be. Some users are so ashamed of their habit that they'll keep it a secret at any cost. But still…I don't think that warrants attacking an FBI agent in an effort to escape."

"Agreed," Kate said, looking at the TV monitor on the wall. Davey still sat there, slightly hunched forward and looking at the floor.

Kate wanted another crack at him—wanted to ask him about the drug use and if there was any connection to his using and the Langleys. Based on what she knew of the Langleys, she doubted there was a connection at all. But any chance to get him to talk about his aunt and uncle would either dig him deeper into the pit or give them just cause to release him.

Before she could start to formulate a line of questioning, though, her cell phone rang. When she saw that it was Duran, she cringed. She knew the man was like a magician at getting details in a quick and timely manner. She wondered if he had somehow found out about her too-rough handling of Davey Armstrong.

"It's Duran," she told DeMarco. She then answered: "This is Wise."

"Where are we on the case?" Duran asked.

"We've got a man in custody right now," Kate said. "I just finished questioning him."

"You think it's the guy?"

"I don't know yet. He's guilty of *something*. Drug use, most likely. But I'm not certain there would be enough to pin the murders on him."

"Send me whatever notes you have, as well as the arrest report. I've got a research issue here in Washington that I could use your help on. One of your old cases that a few agents think might help put an end to a string of kidnappings and a suspected pedophile ring in the Baltimore area. You remember Frank Costello?"

"I do," she said with a chill.

Costello had abducted and killed seven children in 1998, taking them from an area that sprawled between Washington, DC, and Louisville, Kentucky. It was one of the cases that she looked back on as her crowning achievement but, at the same time, an ultimate failure. When Costello had been booked, he claimed to have abducted three more kids and that he had not worked alone. He had never given up the locations of the other three children or the person he claimed to have been working with. That information went with him to the grave, as he killed himself by gnawing open one of his wrists in his cell three days after being caught.

"I'd like you to come meet with this team. So much of what they've come up with mirrors Costello's movements and mannerisms. We can't help but wonder if this latest string of kidnappings is the work of the man Costello says he was working with."

"Yeah, I can be there."

"Good. I thought about just Skyping, but these guys could use you there face to face. A great learning opportunity. So...sorry, Wise. I feel like maybe I overbooked you. If there's more to that case there in Roanoke, do you think DeMarco could handle it on her own?"

"Yeah, I think so."

"Good. Have her send me that info over and get back into town. If you could be here tomorrow, that would be ideal. You good with that?"

Kate looked over at Davey Armstrong on the monitor. If he was the killer, she and DeMarco had wrapped the case much faster than she had expected. If he wasn't, Kate didn't think he'd do much in helping them locate the *actual* killer. But she also didn't think she was in any kind of position to tell Duran no. If she wanted this little deal that they had worked out between them and the bureau, she had to resist any urge to push back.

"That should be fine," she said. "I'll see you tomorrow."

With that, Duran ended the call. Kate pocketed her phone as a thought occurred to her. The story about leaving the pizzas on the porch just seemed too weak. There should be some way to easily find out if it was the truth or not. Maybe a call to Teddy King. Certainly a customer that found their pizzas on their porch would call to complain, right?

"Did you say *see you tomorrow*?" DeMarco asked.

"Yeah. He wants me back in DC. There are some agents who apparently found ties to one of my cold cases about a pedophile ring. I told him I thought you'd be good here."

"I appreciate that," she said, her expression signifying that she meant it.

"Agent DeMarco, would you mind gathering up the police report and making sure a copy is sent to Director Duran as soon as possible? But first maybe we should figure out your car and housing situation."

DeMarco nodded. She looked a little excited at the prospect of being left to run solo on this case but, at the same time, Kate thought she saw a smidge of disappointment.

"You okay?" Kate asked.

"Yeah. I ran cases by myself all the time when I was working violent crimes. And even if Davey Armstrong isn't our man, there's got to be a lead hiding on him or in one of his stories somewhere."

"Maybe," Kate said, but she really didn't think that was going to turn out to be the case at all.

CHAPTER TWELVE

"You know," Kate said as she drove DeMarco to the closest Holiday Inn, "you don't need me to crack this. You're capable of doing it on your own."

"I know," she said. "But if I'm being honest, I just don't like the way Director Duran thinks he can just yank and pull you around like he wants. You went what...a month without him calling at all? And now he sends you out here to check out these murders and then expects you to shift gears and abandon the case at the drop of a hat?"

"Oh, I feel the frustration, too," Kate said. "But there's a really bizarre working arrangement with me coming back from retirement. Until something more concrete is established, I can't rock the boat too much."

"I imagine it's a little easier to be back in DC, though, right?" DeMarco asked. "I mean, with your granddaughter."

"Yeah," Kate said, feeling a sting in her heart when she was reminded of how she had ended her night yesterday.

Hard to think of it as yesterday when I still haven't slept, Kate thought.

"What about you?" Kate asked. "Any reason for you to not want to be around DC?"

"No, not really. I've always liked to travel, so the job suits me. My mom lives in Bethesda, but other than that there's no family around up there. No love interests, either."

"Yeah, you mentioned that on the way down here," Kate said. "And I have to admit...I feel like I need to apologize. I haven't really done a good job in getting to know you. I had no idea you were gay."

DeMarco shrugged. "I'm not the type that lets it define me, you know? I don't have it on my business card or monogrammed on coats or anything. You and I...we just never had a conversation where it came up in a normal fashion."

"I know," Kate said. "And I think that might be because the conversations have always been about me and what it's been like to come out of retirement. Kind of selfish of me."

"No worries at all," DeMarco said. "I can't even imagine trying to stay on this job when you have grandkids. And you've done it *well* for so long."

Kate said nothing, though she wanted to explain to DeMarco that her dedication to her work had been a huge strain on her family. She also kept all thoughts of her husband, Michael, at bay, certainly not wanting to tell her that even after Michael had been killed, work had come first. It had simply been something she had never been able to unhinge herself from.

"You said your mom lives in Bethesda," Kate said. "Are you guys close?"

"I suppose. We've never been really tight or anything. But I'm all she's got, as sad as that sounds, so I suppose we're close enough."

DeMarco looked blankly out of the windshield as she briefly discussed her mother. She spoke quickly and in a flat tone as well. To Kate, it was a nonverbal and polite way of saying *I'd really rather not talk about it.*

As the Holiday Inn sign came into view, Kate felt a feeling of guilt for the first time. Was she abandoning DeMarco? Sure, she was only following Duran's orders but still…they had come here together to attempt to solve these murders and here she was, barely over twelve hours later, about to head back without her.

"Please don't hesitate to call me with any new information. If this thing starts to escalate, I imagine Duran would send me back to assist."

"I'll keep that in mind, but I think I'll be okay," DeMarco said.

"Want me to call ahead to a car rental place?" Kate asked.

"Nah, I'll delegate that to the police. Maybe I'll get Palmetto to do it."

Kate chuckled as she pulled into the parking lot of the Holiday Inn. "I fully expect you to have this wrapped up by the time I return home," she said with a smile.

"We can't all knock cases out of the park like Kate Wise," DeMarco said. "But thanks for the vote of confidence."

Kate parked in front of the motel. She had been here before, stuck in limbo without knowing exactly where she was going to stay or how she was going to get from Point A to Point B. She remembered that part of her career fondly, particularly a case out in Utah where she had been stranded for two days because her rental car had broken down and there had been some miscommunication between the bureau and the airport. She did miss those days and she envied DeMarco a bit.

"Be careful and take care," Kate said.

"Says the fifty-five-year-old that threw a flying tackle on Davey Armstrong three hours ago," DeMarco said.

With a grin and a nod, DeMarco got out of the car. She gave one final wave as she headed in through the lobby doors and then disappeared inside.

Kate checked the time and saw that somehow, it was only 4:47 in the afternoon. She was no longer truly tired, having been reinvigorated by coffee and finding her second wind after chasing down Davey Armstrong. If she drove straight through without stopping, she figured she could be back home sometime around 8:30. She could sleep the night through and wake up around seven in the morning to call Duran to see how she could help with the research job.

While she hated to leave a case when it had not yet been officially closed, she also could not deny that it felt very good to feel wanted—to feel *needed* in a job that had once so strongly defined her.

Still, that promise of normal life shone bright. It was what caused her to pull out her phone and send a quick text to Melissa before pulling back out of the parking lot. She thought about what to say for several seconds and, after some trial and error, finally decided on something simple and to the point: **Sorry about last night. Can we meet sometime Monday?**

She honestly wasn't expecting a response, but she figured she had to at least try. And as she pulled back out onto the street and in the direction of DC, she tried to imagine how to explain herself to Melissa. What the hell was she supposed to say? *Sorry, sweetie...but that job that took so much of your childhood away from me is already starting to do the same with my granddaughter, too.*

It was miserable and it broke her heart, but God help her, she worried that it was going to end up being the truth.

CHAPTER THIRTEEN

Kate managed to keep the pull of exhaustion away up until she got on the exit that would lead her into Richmond. There, she let out a yawn so long and deep that she could practically already feel her bed beneath her. She had estimated her time almost perfectly, finally coasting slowly down the streets of Carytown toward her house at 8:40.

Still, despite being somewhere beyond tired, she could not stop thinking about DeMarco. Kate had always had a habit of not wanting to stop working on a case until a final, official, and unbreakable arrest had been made. Naturally, she felt as if she had left the murdered couples' case long before it had been truly wrapped up; she knew it would nag at her until the case was closed. And while she trusted DeMarco to get the job done, Kate Wise had never enjoyed feeling as if she had given up on something.

She found a parking spot close to her house and felt like she was sleepwalking as she walked from her car to her front porch. She was so tired that she had made it all the way up the porch steps before she saw the man on her porch. He was sitting in one of her little faux Adirondack chairs, smiling sheepishly at her.

It was Allen. And despite the thin smile, Kate could tell that he was hurt.

Shit, she thought. *We were supposed to go out for dinner tonight. And I totally forgot.*

She walked over to him and plopped herself down in the chair beside his. They'd sat like this on her porch a few times before. There had usually been a glass of wine in her hand, and a beer in his. But now there was none of that. Now, she knew she had dropped the ball and needed to apologize.

"Allen, I'm so sorry," she said. "I got a call last night from the bureau. They sent me out to Roanoke on this rush thing and…and I just plain forgot."

"It's okay," he said. Allen looked at his watch and added: "I was going to give you until nine and then head back home. I figured it had something to do with your daughter, granddaughter, or work."

"Why didn't you call to remind me?" she asked.

Not that it would have mattered, Kate thought. *All that would have accomplished was making me feel guilty while trying to find a killer.*

Allen shrugged. "Because I knew it wasn't my place. I know that you have a life. A very busy life. I don't say this looking for pity, but I know I'm not on the list of high priorities. And I'm fine with that. It's the sort of relationship I need in my life right now."

"That's not fair to you," Kate said. "How long have you been waiting here?"

"Two hours. But it's cool. It was a nice break. I read some news on my phone, got to play on my Sudoku app, too. At the risk of sounding cheesy, I like it on your porch. It makes me happy. It makes me happier when you're on it with me, but I'll take what I can get."

Kate reached out and took his hand. "Have you had dinner yet?"

"No."

"Come inside. We can whip something up together."

He gave her hand a squeeze and chuckled. "Kate, I'm not sure where you've been and what you've been doing, but you look exhausted. Go in and get some sleep. We can do this some other time."

"No. Look...yes, I'm running on zero sleep for the last day and a half or so. But I want to see you. So why don't you figure out what you want to eat and call it in. I'll grab a shower really quick and we can head out and just pick it up."

"Or we could have it delivered here," he said. "If you don't mind me hanging around, of course."

"That sounds like a plan," she said.

She bit her lip when she nearly found herself inviting him into the shower with her after he made the call for the food. The thought of it excited her but no man had seen her naked since Michael died nearly six years ago. It had been a long stretch of time and while she desperately wanted some kind of physical intimacy again, she wasn't sure if she could be so blatant and inviting about it.

"Go take your shower," he said with more than a hint of suggestiveness in his eyes. "I'll be on the way to pick up our food when you get out. It'll be quicker than waiting for it to be delivered."

"Thanks for understanding," Kate said. She leaned in and kissed him slowly. They had kissed many times—often, actually—but there had never been one that had left her feeling lightheaded.

This one did it, but it might have been because closing her eyes reminded her of just how tired she was.

"Are you okay, Kate? You look more than tired. You look...I don't know. Troubled?"

A million things went through Kate's mind in that moment: an image of Michelle on her bed, looking up at her with hopeful and expectant eyes; Davey Armstrong sitting in a holding cell in Roanoke; the bloodstains on the Nashes' living room floor; the hateful and hurt look on Melissa's face as she walked away with Michelle in the car seat.

"I'll be okay," Kate said. "I think the shower will help."

With that, she headed back inside. She felt herself wanting to cry, something that she rarely did. Maybe a shower would wake her up a bit but as far as all of the other things swimming around in her head, no shower of any warmth or length would be able to wash it all away.

***

Allen was setting the table when she came out of her bedroom. The shower, getting dressed, and making some sense out of her wet hair had taken a little less than half an hour. In that time, Allen had apparently decided to just walk three blocks down to the street to the Italian deli. He knew her order there—a traditional meatball sub—and he had it on her plate when she came in.

The shower *had* helped a bit in terms of how tired she was. But she knew she'd crash soon. It wasn't much of a date but she was glad to see Allen at all, especially after the way the last twenty-four hours of her life had gone.

"I know we have this dinner a lot," Allen said, plopping his pastrami sandwich down on his plate. "But it was getting late and I didn't want you to stay up any later than you had to."

"No, this is perfect," she said. She started eating right away, having not had anything of substance since the pizza at Gino's. And that was already starting to feel like a lifetime ago.

They ate in silence for about three minutes before Allen spoke up. When he did, Kate could tell that he was very hesitant to ask his question. She respected him for going there, for asking the tough questions to make sure she was okay.

"Do you want to talk about it?" he asked. "Whatever it is that had you called away...I can listen, you know?"

"I know," she said. "But the case isn't closed yet, so I'm not supposed to give out any pertinent information. You understand that, right?"

"Absolutely. So, if it was such a rush sort of job, what brought you back so soon?"

She did her best to explain the situation, letting him know that she was needed for some type of research role to help bring a high-profile local case to a close. As she did, she started to understand how self-obsessed she must seem to him. Leaving her granddaughter and ending her daughter's night out...dropping everything right away just so she could recapture a feeling of purpose.

God, have I always been like this? she wondered as she finished up her explanation and the table fell to silence again.

With dinner eaten and conversation at a stand-still, Allen stood up and cleared their plates and the take-out containers. "Off to bed you. Do you need a wake-up call in the morning? You look like you're going to sleep pretty hard."

That same spark she'd felt when she had nearly asked him to come into the shower with her reignited. This time, she did not ignore it. Maybe if she had not been so tired she would have put up more of a mental block against it.

"Yeah, a wake-up call would be good," she said. She got up and walked over to him as he put the dishes into the sink. "So at about seven in the morning, I need you to roll over and shake me a bit."

He didn't bother playing dumb. He just gave her a curious look and smiled. "You sure?"

"I am," she said. To punctuate this, she stepped forward and placed her hands on his waist. She pulled him to her and kissed him softly but with a deep passion she had not felt in a very long time.

He responded in kind and somehow, she ended up with her back pressed against the sink. She had to stop the kiss just to catch her breath.

With his face still directly in front of hers, their lips no more than an inch apart, he looked into her eyes. "This will be the last time I ask," he said. "I'm trying to be polite but I'm still a man and all. Are you sure?"

She gently pushed him away from her and walked to the kitchen window. She closed the blinds and then turned to face him. That done, she reached up to the top button of her shirt and undid it. The second one followed. As she started working on the third, she looked up at him with what she hoped was a seductive stare.

"This would go quicker if you would lend a hand."

Allen, as it turned out, was happy to oblige. He walked quickly over to her and in the whirlwind of another of those kisses, helped her finish the task.

***

Before Michael, Kate had only slept with two men. That made Allen the fourth. And as she stirred awake at three in the morning, she tried to recall if she had ever climaxed as hard as she had the night before. She'd reached it twice and the second one had been so powerful that it had scared her a bit. Thinking back on it in that three a.m. darkness, she smiled to herself. She rolled over and looked at Allen, sleeping as peacefully as she had hoped to.

But sleep had been tricky. First, her nerves had remained on fire when she and Allen had finished. It hadn't lasted long and they had both fallen into bed quite tired. But her body had remained amped up until almost eleven and then she had come awake just after three with the images of the bodies of the Langleys in her mind. She saw them as she had only ever seen them, in the glossy portrait paper within the case files. Bloodied, massacred...and for what?

Then, for reasons she was not clear on, she started ruminating on the case that had attacked her memory leaving a Carytown shop two days ago. Something about that case would not leave her alone. At the end, a little girl had been saved and a man who had been actively killing people at an alarming speed had been brought to justice.

Only, that really wasn't the case, she thought in the darkness with Allen beside her. Her director at the time had insisted that they had their man even though some of the evidence had been questionable at best. They'd called the case a wrap and then, after that little girl had been returned safely home, two more kids had been found murdered a month later in another state. They'd eventually found the *real* killer, but Kate had never forgiven herself for ignoring her instincts—for not arguing against her former director when she had felt that the man they had apprehended was not the killer.

As quietly as she could, she got out of bed and walked into the kitchen. She got a glass of water and sat in her recliner, thinking back about that case—thinking about DeMarco and a man she was now starting to think was not guilty at all.

"You okay?"

She turned and saw Allen standing in the doorway of the bedroom. He had put his boxers back on but the rest of his body was bare. He looked damned good for a fifty-four-year-old and her mind, if only briefly, jumped away from the darker things she had been dwelling on and to the activities of about five hours ago.

"Yeah. I just couldn't sleep."

"Is it bad? Like, can I make a joke about you coming back to bed and us not sleeping at all?"

She smiled and moved toward him. "Make any jokes you want," she said. "So long as you're ready to back them up."

And before he could make another comment, she was kissing him and leading him back to her bed.

CHAPTER FOURTEEN

Seven miles away from where a man named David "Davey" Armstrong lay half-asleep on a cot in a holding cell, another man woke up quickly in bed. He stared at the digital numbers of his alarm clock and saw that it was 5:05. He had an internal alarm that had been waking him up at this time ever since he'd been a child—as early as the age of ten.

Like an automated machine, he got out of bed, took six steps to the rug in front of his bed (six steps which he counted under his breath every morning), and assumed a push-up position. He blasted through one hundred push-ups and then immediately went to the shower. He scrubbed himself and washed his short black hair with the same machine-like mannerisms in which he had gotten out of bed and exercised.

Five minutes later he was toweling off as he walked back into his bedroom. He dressed quickly for the day, a black T-shirt and a faded pair of jeans, and walked into the kitchen. He saw that it was 5:27 and frowned. He was two minutes off. He lived his days by a very strict schedule and even two minutes off could make or break his mood.

And this morning, he was in a very good mood. He felt good—better than he had in quite some time. Maybe that was why he was in the kitchen two minutes early. After all, he'd been on a very busy schedule for the last week or so.

He sat down at his kitchen table with a bowl of cereal and scrolled through Facebook on his iPhone. As usual, he saw nothing of interest. Trump had said something dumb again. Some racist person said something racist. People were posting little videos of cats and cute kids and women in swimsuits that showed everything.

He smirked at it all as he ate his cereal. He cast his thoughts to later in the day—not when he was supposed to head into work, but to some task he had set for himself beyond his monotonous job. He worked at a small plastics factory on the far side of town, pushing buttons, snipping wire, and repeating it a trillion times. He loathed the job but it gave him ample time to think. It gave him the opportunity to think back on his past and figure out where everything had gone so terribly wrong.

Of course, other than his father killing his mother, he could come up with nothing. And he'd been so young when that happened...maybe there had been something else as he'd gotten older.

He spent some of his time at work trying to think of the first time the darkness had entered his mind—when he'd first had those violent and bloody thoughts. But nothing concrete ever came to him.

But he didn't like to dwell there very often. It made him feel like there was something wrong with him. So he turned his thoughts back to all of the wonderful things he had been doing in his spare time lately. That always got him in a much better mood. He figured if he could keep it up and be done with it within a few more days he might actually be able to become a better person. He might finally be able to put the past behind him.

Done with his cereal, he placed the bowl in the sink and headed back to his room. He had fifteen more minutes before he needed to be at work. Usually he would read when he had down time but he had been too busy and distracted to read as of late. Instead of pulling one of his books from the stack along the side of his bed, he reached under his bed and pulled out the shoebox.

Up until recently, the lid of the shoebox had been coated with a layer of fine dust. But he had brushed the dust off two weeks ago and started to dwell on what was inside. As a matter of fact, the things that were inside the shoebox had been consuming his thoughts as of late.

He pried the lid from the box with deliberate care and smiled at what he saw inside.

He took out the stuffed animal, a little gray rabbit with one ear droopy and the other standing at attention. It smiled dumbly up at him with its little glass eyes. And even though he was now an adult, that goofy smile made him feel safe and secure—like there was someone or something in this fucked up world that actually cared for him.

He placed the rabbit on his bed and looked back into the box. There was one more thing in there, which he took out with the same loving care he had showed the rabbit.

He handled the blanket in a way that was childlike, as if he might lie back down on his bed with it and snuggle up to its tattered shape.

Instead, he held it up by its torn edge and started to tear it. It gave way easy, just as it had done the two other times he had torn a strip from it.

He looked at the new fragment of the blanket and smiled. He was tempted to do it now, to do the job in the morning. He could call in sick to work and just do it. But no...he liked having the day to wait, to build up the excitement.

He placed the box back under the bed with its contents returned. All except that one scrap of fabric which he laid in the center of his bed. He stared longingly at it for a moment before leaving the room to get his day started.

CHAPTER FIFTEEN

It was beyond bizarre to wake up with someone on the opposite side of the bed. Kate took a moment to appreciate the feeling as she quietly got out of bed. She grabbed a pair of underwear and her robe and snuck out of the room while Allen still slept. It made her feel a little immature, but she could not get over how happy she was. She hadn't had a man sleep over since Michael had died. There was something freeing about it—something that made her remember that it was okay to live a little selfishly from time to time.

She walked into the kitchen and started brewing a pot of coffee. She then cracked a few eggs and started making some omelets. As the coffee brewed and the eggs cooked, she impulsively went to the kitchen counter and opened her iPad, pulling up the files on the case in Roanoke. As was her usual approach, she knew she would not be able to stop thinking about the case until it was one hundred percent officially wrapped up.

She looked for any details she might have missed but there were none. She knew that as the coroners finished up their jobs and forensics had everything submitted, there would be more to go on. But for now, she felt that she and DeMarco had done just about everything they could. Still, that did nothing to eliminate the fact that she could not get over the feeling that they were missing something—something that was right in front of their faces.

Kate closed down the files and then opened up her email. She had several, all of which were related to the research assistance she had lined up later in the day. It seemed very cut-and-dried and, if the agents she was overseeing worked well together, they should be able to have their current case wrapped very quickly. She also saw that she was being asked to be in DC by three that afternoon. She read over the case brief that had been put together for her, reading it twice and committing it to memory. It really did seem like a case that was one good theory or lead away from being wrapped up.

She heard footsteps behind her. Before she could turn around, she felt Allen's hands on her shoulders, gently massaging her. He kissed her on the back of the neck, sending a delightful chill through her.

"Good morning," he said.

"Good morning to you, too," she said. She clicked the iPad to sleep as she turned to face him.

"You shut the iPad down right away," he said. "Sensitive information?"

"Sort of," she said. "You hungry?"

He looked to the bar where she had set their plates. She had slightly burned the omelets because she'd been distracted with the case files but she didn't think Allen was the type who would complain about such a thing.

"Absolutely," he said.

He walked to the barstool along the counter, dressed in the same clothes he'd been wearing last night. He had a look on his face that mirrored Kate's own feelings. She was starting to think that Allen very rarely found himself in these sorts of situations, either.

"Are you going back to it all because you miss it or just because retirement isn't your thing?" Allen asked, nodding toward the iPad.

"I ask myself that almost every day," she said. "It's mostly because I miss it. It's all I was ever good at."

"After last night, I beg to differ," he said with a sly little smile.

She turned away a bit as her cheeks flushed. "Anyway, I need to be in DC by three o'clock this afternoon. It'll probably be a pretty quick trip if you want to try to make some plans for tomorrow."

"Yeah, that sounds good to me," he said, cutting into his breakfast.

"Sorry again that I made you wait so long last night."

"Oh, that's okay," he said. "Really. Part of me is a little enamored with what you do. I'd like for you to not tell me any different, but I imagine you kicking in doors and wrestling perps to the ground. It's sort of hot."

She couldn't contain her smile when she thought of tackling Davey Armstrong to the ground yesterday. "Yes, sure," she said. "It's like that for me just about every day. Lots of running and tackling."

"So," he said, forking up the last bit of omelet, "if you're supposed to be in DC at three, I guess you need to get a move on, huh?"

"Yeah, I probably should get ready."

"Am I a terrible guest if I ask if I can use your shower before I head out?" Allen asked.

"Not at all," she said. "Give me some time and maybe I'll join you."

Now it was his turn to hide a little redness in his cheeks. He placed his plate in the sink and took one last sip of his coffee before heading out of the kitchen. He placed a small kiss on the corner of her mouth and headed back toward the bedroom.

Kate did fully intend to join him, but her mind instantly went back to the case. She kept seeing those pieces of fabric, portions of a blanket that had been shoved into the mouths of the victims. She looked to the clock over the kitchen sink, saw that it was 8:37, and decided to call DeMarco.

She answered on the second ring and sounded pleased that Kate had called. "It's feeling pretty lonesome down here in Roanoke," DeMarco said.

"Nothing new?"

"Nothing. I've even gone so far as to check high school records for the Nashes and the Langleys, hoping to find some sort of connection. I also requested all of the forms and paperwork from the county that concern anything to do with the Langleys' foster care process. I'll be getting that today but based on what the Department of Social Services thinks, the Langleys are pretty much perfect. No criminal records or red flags of any kind. So I'm not expecting to find skeletons in their closet."

"And the Nashes were never foster parents, right?"

"Not from what we have. There's nothing that points there, anyway. That *would* be a pretty notable link, though, wouldn't it?"

"Yes, but if it's not there, it's not there." She sighed and then added: "How about Davey Armstrong? Everyone down there still seem to think it's him?"

"Yeah, and there's at least *some* evidence to back it. It's not as strong as I'd like, but it's enough to keep him for a while. For instance, there's a police record from when Davey was seventeen. He locked himself in the Langleys' bathroom with a handgun and was threatening to kill himself. There are also some pretty bad G-chat messages that were just found last night on his computer. He was talking to some friend of his from the community college about his experiences with the Langleys. He talks about some pretty sick sex fantasies about Bethany Langley. He mentioned rape a few times."

"You think you can send them to me?" Kate asked.

"Yeah, if you want."

"Anything else?"

"No, that's about it. I spoke with the college friend about those messages and he swears he doesn't think Davey would have it in him to kill anyone. He *did* say that Davey seemed a little spacey at times, though. To tell you the truth, I can see Duran calling me back up to DC tomorrow if nothing else big breaks on this thing."

"Well, keep me posted," Kate said. "Let me know if you need anything."

They ended the call and Kate instantly tried to think of Davey Armstrong as a teen, living in the Langleys' house and harboring sexual fantasies about his aunt. That added item made the whole thing a little different. Maybe there *was* something Davey wasn't telling them. Maybe he was ashamed not only about the drug use, but about the way he'd felt about his aunt as well.

The idea of it made her uncomfortable. And although she had told Allen she might join him in the shower, any thoughts of sexual activity were erased from her mind with this new update about Davey Armstrong. Instead of joining Allen, she remained at the counter, poring over the files once again and sipping from her coffee.

What the hell am I missing? she asked herself, sure that there was something there right in front of her that had somehow eluded her so far.

***

Allen didn't comment on Kate deciding not to join him in the shower. He seemed to understand that her mind was usually never on one single track, but all over the place. Kate figured that if they were going to eventually explore a longer relationship later on, this might be something they'd have to tackle head on. But for now, she simply appreciated the fact that he was understanding.

She had started packing when he came out of the bathroom. His pants were on and he was toweling off his hair.

"You okay with this?" he asked.

"With what?" she asked.

He shrugged as he slid his shirt on. "Well, last night was amazing, don't get me wrong. But now the coming and going and your busy life. I don't know. I feel like maybe I used you or something. Maybe I took advantage of your busy schedule and situation. Is that stupid?"

"No," she said, her heart warming for him. "If anything, it's incredibly sweet. No, you did not use me. And I didn't do it out of guilt from making you wait, either. So don't bother going there."

"Good to know," he said. "You mind if I hang around until you leave?"

"Not at all."

Within a few minutes, he was in the kitchen washing the dishes from breakfast. He helped himself to another cup of coffee and sat with her in the bedroom while she packed. They had a pleasant enough conversation about surface-level things: the week's forecast, restaurants they'd like to try, movies they might see together in the theater in the coming weeks. As far as Kate was concerned, it was nice to have such innocent and mundane conversations.

She was packed up and heading for the door by 9:30. That would put her in DC at least two hours before she was due there, but that was fine with her. She figured she might try to catch up with Duran to discuss the case in Roanoke.

Allen carried her one bag out for her and placed it in the trunk of her car. He then reached out and took her hand.

"I like this," he said. "This, of course, not having a definition. Whatever it is that's going on between us...I like it."

"I do, too," she said. "I'll call you when I'm on the way home."

"You don't have to. I promise I won't wait sadly on your porch until you get back."

"But I want to," she said. She nearly voiced the reasoning behind it, but let it remain in her head instead. *I like the idea that someone is waiting for me, someone who is looking forward to seeing me again.*

With that thought in mind, she also realized that Melissa had yet to return her text. This pained her, but she could not focus on it right now.

Then when? she asked herself as Allen opened the car door for her. *If you want that relationship to work, you need to face it sooner rather than later.*

She got into the car with a heavy sigh, trying to ease the storm in her head.

"You okay?" Allen asked.

"Yeah. Just a lot on my mind. Work...Melissa...I really am just a big mess. You'll figure it out pretty soon, I guess."

He smiled at her, leaned into the car, and kissed her. The kiss carried some heat and it had her buzzing in all the right spots. When he pulled away, God help her, she was lightheaded.

"Be careful out there," Allen said.

"I'll try. See you soon."

He closed her door and gave her a little wave as she started the car. When she pulled off, she looked back and saw him still watching from the sidewalk. She smiled at the sight of him and, for the first time in a very long time, wondered if maybe there *was* something to life other than the niche she had carved out for herself at work. Sure, there were Melissa and Michelle, but there was also this unnamable thing between her and Allen. Not love, not yet anyway, but some sort of tug that felt like being wanted.

That, in tandem with knowing that she would get to watch little Michelle grow up, made her feel an intense joy that caught her off guard. It was something she had not felt in a very long time—something other than her job that actually had her excited for the future.

CHAPTER SIXTEEN

Kate had to admit…it felt good to be back around the mild chaos and business of DC. The moment her eyes fell on the J. Edgar Hoover building, she felt a sense of well-being that she had rarely felt at home following her retirement. She had spent so much time there, had etched out a name and a legacy for herself in that building. It brought back more than memories; it brought back a feeling of purpose and accomplishment that she had been struggling to find back at home in Richmond.

She'd hit a snag in traffic so had not arrived as early as she had hoped. Therefore, she parked in the same parking garage she had parked in for nearly thirty years of her life (of course, it had been updated—modified and added to a lot in those three decades) and headed straight into the building. It was never truly empty, but it was the closest to vacant as it ever was on Sundays. She passed by only five people on her way to the second floor where one of the larger conference rooms had been reserved for the meeting.

When she stepped into the room twenty minutes early, she was pleased to see that a few members of the investigative unit were already there. A projector had been set up and the Keurig on the back table was purring as it filled a cup with coffee. She noticed right away that several of the members of the team looked tired, an indication that they had been putting countless extra hours into this case. She knew the look well; it meant that the case was either on the verge of being cracked or that they were throwing one last Hail Mary attempt at closing it.

"Agent Wise," a tall-statured woman from the front of the room said. "Thank you so much for agreeing to meet with us."

Rather than letting this woman know that Duran had really not given her much of a choice, Kate simply said, "Of course," and shook the woman's hand when it was offered.

The six other agents and assistants in the room also made their way over to her, introducing themselves and giving their thanks. Midway through this, Duran entered the room. He looked like he was in a hurry as usual but also looked satisfied that everyone was present and accounted for a full ten minutes before the meeting was set to begin.

He gave a quick nod around the room and then motioned Kate forward. "Can I see you outside for a moment?" he asked.

She followed him out into the hall, taking note that he closed the door behind them.

"This team is made up of agents who have less than five years of experience each," Duran explained to her. "But they all had tremendous results in the academy and, I believe, have the potential to be great agents with legacies *maybe* as stellar as yours. I tell you all of this so you can understand how motivated they are. They are extremely close to catching this guy and, as I explained earlier, a lot of what they've come up with mirrors the Frank Costello case. You remember the details well enough to help?"

"I remember the details of the Costello case a little *too* vividly."

"Good. Help them out but don't demean them. You're here as support, not as a teacher. But, at the same time, if you could manage to lead them to where you think the path needs to lead…"

She nodded. "I understand."

When they stepped back into the conference room, the team of seven were sitting around the table. Five of them were on devices—laptops, their phones, or tablets. Two preferred the old-school approach and were at the ready with pen and paper.

"So," she said as she claimed one of the three free seats at the table. "I've read over the case brief and am up to speed on the amazing work you all have done. But who would like to tell me how you got here? How are you this close to bringing this guy in?"

A sleek-looking man who looked to be in his late twenties took the cue. He didn't even let the others *think* about answering her question. Kate tried to decide if he was a kiss-ass or just extremely dedicated.

"Four kidnappings in the last three weeks," this man said. "One in Bethesda, Maryland, two outside of Fredericksburg, Virginia, and the other two in Louisville, Kentucky. There have been no bodies and no letters from the abductor. No demands. Which, honestly, is almost as bad as finding a body."

Kate didn't agree with this, but she understood where he was coming from. If there were no demands being made for the release of the children, there was no telling what they were going through.

As the sleek-looking man paused, the tall woman who had introduced herself to Kate spoke up. "Obviously, the area of interest mirrors the same locations as Frank Costello…not to a tee, but too close to ignore. Also, like Frank Costello, there is no preference of boys or girls. So far, two of each have been abducted."

"Walk me through each potential abduction scene," Kate said.

Another woman took this one. She sounded nervous and tired. "Two were taken from playgrounds, while the mothers were there with them. One of them admits to scrolling through Facebook while her kid was on the monkey bars. She guesses that there was perhaps fifteen to twenty seconds between her peering up from her screen. The third seems to have been taken after straying a bit away from her father in a Walmart in Louisville. The fourth had been walking to her grandmother's house, just six houses down the street from her own home. She'd done it dozens of times, according to her mother."

"Not a single witness at all," the sleek man said. "Somehow, we don't even have this fucker leaving that Walmart on the security cameras."

"How's that possible?" Kate asked.

"Lawn and garden," one of the agents said. "There's only one security camera in the lawn and garden department of that particular Walmart. It faces in from the open air area of the flower section. If someone knew the layout of the store well enough, they would know how to make an exit through lawn and garden without being seen."

Kate's brain was already kicking into high gear, trying to put the pieces together. "Have you checked past employees with knowledge of the camera systems?"

"We've interviewed eleven," the tall woman said. "Two were questioned a second time. In the end, it all came down to nothing."

Kate took a moment, getting out of her seat and walking to the front of the room. "If the presumption is that this man is connected to Frank Costello, it's not even necessarily the locations that would matter—though it *is* very odd about the security cameras. We have to think like Frank Costello thought. Have you all looked at the footage from his interrogations?"

"Several times," a particularly tired-looking man at the back of the table said.

"We've looked at the profiles of the kids, of the families, of even the fucking grandparents," an angry-looking hefty man on the other side of the table said. "But there doesn't seem to be anything."

"The thing that ended up tripping Frank Costello wasn't any of that," Kate said. "You're looking in the wrong place if you think you're going to catch this guy by hoping he's using the same methodologies as Costello. Instead, you have to look at where Costello messed up. And as the files show you, the thing that led him to us in the end was the smallest of details—a small thing that connected each of the families not in genetics or daily routines, but in something so trivial it was never even looked at until it smacked me right in the face."

"You mean the YMCA," the tall female agent said.

"Hey, that's right," the sleek agent said. He now looked very pleased that he was in the room. He was also looking at Kate with the same sort of reverence that most younger agents had when she had been filling out the last of her days as an on-duty agent. "You found out in the end that the parents of those kids all had memberships to the YMCA. Costello was a member, too. But that's really not too remarkable because *tons* of people have memberships to the YMCA."

"Exactly," Kate said. She paused for a moment when she realized that every eye in the room was on her—even the pair in Duran's head. He was smiling approvingly at her as he nodded for her to go on. "Costello used the YMCA as his hunting grounds. He scoped out the gyms—for about seven months, according to his story. He even played a few games of pick-up racquetball with the father of one of his victims."

"So we need to be looking for links outside of the basic family aspects of it all," another of the agents said. "But I don't even know if there *are* any. If so, we would have stumbled across it by now."

"Maybe you have," Kate said. "Maybe it was right there in front of you the entire time but it looked so mundane and ordinary that you looked past it. Frank Costello did not adjust his life when he started abducting kids. He never stopped going to the YMCA and he never quit his job—never took any extra sick days or anything. And if we know that about him and we also know that he was working with someone else..."

"Then they're probably doing the same things," the sleek agent said.

"But why wait nearly twenty years to start again?" the angry-looking agent asked, typing something into his laptop without looking up.

"Maybe it took that long for him to work up the nerve," Duran suggested. "He's never done this on his own before."

"It's pretty much a textbook example of a man who's been left behind by a partner in this kind of thing," Kate said. "When Costello was apprehended and their little adventures came to an end, whatever partner he had likely found himself lost. A *now what?* sort of mentality. But something like abducting and killing kids...that just doesn't go away. So yes...maybe it *was* just a matter of working up the nerve to get back to it. It's likely, even. But we have to think about the sorts of things he might have been harboring or even putting into practice during that time. If he's like Costello, he's likely trying to *not* stand out. He's not interrupting his daily life. And that's a plus for you because that means he should be leaving a pretty big footprint. We just need to know where to start looking."

"Yes, and that's where we're coming up empty," the tall female agent said. "When you've got a guy that moves around like a phantom, it's hard to pin him down. We've checked security cameras, traffic cameras…"

"We even had a team of agents check security camera footage of every gas station within twenty miles of each abduction site for *anything* we could find," the formerly angry man said. "And *nothing*."

"Have you checked over the sites of Costello's abductions?" Kate asked.

"No use," the sleek-looking agent said. "Of the two for-sure sites, one is a street that has now basically been bulldozed and turned into a high-end community. The other was a small playground that has gone to rot."

"But you know," the female agent said thoughtfully, "you mentioned normal things a moment ago. About looking into things that are so obvious you overlook them until they slap you in the face…"

She then started to rapidly flip through the pages of a case file in front of her. Without looking up, she said, "Lockridge, do you have the findings from the playground the third victim was taken from?"

"Yeah," the sleek-looking agent said. He clicked around on his laptop for a few seconds and added: "What are you looking for?"

"The waste basket from the corner of the playground. It had been recently emptied, and the man from grounds maintenance believed anything in that can could have not been any older than five or six hours. You have the list of what was in there?"

"Two Coke cans, a flier for a local business, an empty bag of ranch-flavored peanuts, a cracked sippy cup with a picture of Elmo on it."

The female agent pulled a sheet of paper from her pile and slammed it on the table with such force that a few of the others huddled around the table jumped. "Right here," she said, excited. "The fourth victim, taken presumably while she was walking to her grandmother's house. Remember what forensics said they found in the street?"

"Holy shit," one agent said.

"Wait, let's not assume," Lockridge said.

"Nuts of some kind, probably prepackaged," the woman said. "Not cashews but something similar."

Kate had been in rooms where an *a-ha* moment had been reached. The feeling of electricity in the air never got old. She felt it rustling through the conference room in that moment as the team of agents shared looks of acknowledgment or stared at their laptop screens at the information they had accumulated.

Sensing that she had more or less started rolling a small snowball down a steep hill, Kate went on.

"So you start there. Go back to those gas stations and convenience stores. Some of them will likely be able to pull transaction records from as far back as a month. Align each purchase of those nuts to the security footage. That will give you a handful of suspects. After that…"

"They can cross that bridge when they get there," Duran said. "For now, Agent Wise, if you wouldn't mind just giving them a quick criminal profile on Frank Costello."

"Of course," she said. She reached back into her nearly flawless memory and saw the information from the case file. It was one that had stuck with her, as it had been pivotal to her career.

Yet, even as she started detailing the trouble childhood that Frank Costello had endured, Kate's mind went back to Roanoke. She started to once again focus on the murders that were taking place there. She had said something moments ago that was just now setting something ablaze in her mind.

"Maybe it was right there in front of you the entire time but it looked so mundane and ordinary that you looked past it."

This thought swirled at the edges of her mind for the next half an hour as she told the room everything she knew about how Frank Costello had carried out his abductions and murders. Combined with the breakthrough she'd assisted with moments ago, she had no doubts that this highly capable team would have someone in custody within forty-eight hours.

When she called the meeting to a close, the agents got up from the table quickly, anxious to get back out on the trail. Yet as everyone else cleared out, the tall woman hung back. She approached Kate with a look of apprehension as she slung her laptop bag over her shoulder.

"Agent Wise," she said. "I had to take the moment to introduce myself. My name is Rebecca Minor. I've been admiring your work since I first joined the academy. You're the sole reason I wanted to pursue a career as a field agent rather than a lab tech, which is what I was originally going to be."

"Thank you," Kate said, not sure how to take such a compliment.

"I have to admit…I have a lot of your archived case files printed out and in a binder at home. I used them as study guides while I was at the academy."

"Well, it seems that they helped. You're doing a fantastic job from what I can see. You'll have this guy sooner than you think. You're on the right path, you know. Just let it—"

Her phone buzzed in her pocket, interrupting her. She gave an *I'm sorry* look to Agent Minor as she checked it. When she saw that the call was coming from DeMarco, she smiled wanly at Minor and turned away. She marched quickly to the back of the room and took the call.

"Hi, DeMarco. How's it going?"

"Well, it could be better. He did it again."

"The killer?"

"Yeah…"

Kate looked back across the room to where Duran was still standing by the door. He saw her looking and the glance exchanged between them communicated everything. Before she even ended the call with DeMarco, Kate knew that she was heading back to Roanoke.

CHAPTER SEVENTEEN

Kate felt a sense of unease spreading through her as she entered the driveway of the third murder scene. From the sight of the house alone, she could tell that there was something different about this one—that the killer had to have been incredibly motivated to strike here.

First of all, the house was gorgeous. It was an enormous house, done in an altered Colonial style. The grass was perfectly cut and green, bordering the porch like something out of a gardening magazine. Behind the house, she could see the edge of a pond peeking out. The house was situated up on a hill, as if whoever lived inside felt the need to look out on top of the city of Roanoke, which sat to the east as just a tangle of shapes against the trees.

It would have been a beautiful sight indeed if not for the presence of the two police cars and the black sedan. The sedan, she knew, was what DeMarco was driving. Kate parked behind the sedan and walked toward the house. As she made her way up the porch stairs, a policeman came out of the front door. She wasn't too surprised to see that it was Palmetto. He looked tired but managed a smile when he saw her.

"Agent Wise," he said. "Good to see you again."

"Likewise," she said. "You headed out?"

"Yeah. I'm going to see if I can help relieve you guys of some of the monotony. I'm going to see what I can find out from family and friends of the newly deceased. Going to get a few of the local officers to assist. I'll meet back up with you guys later today."

"Thanks for that," Kate said as she headed inside the house.

"Sure." He regarded her with a strange look that made her think he meant to say something else. But he simply returned to his car and started the engine.

Kate made her way into the house and quickly discovered that the interior was just as beautiful as the exterior. The front door led to a tall foyer that showed the full staircase leading upstairs. It was there, looking at her out over the railing, that DeMarco stood. A trail of drying blood led up the stairs to her, stopping at a crumpled shape at DeMarco's feet.

"How long have you been on the scene?" Kate asked, carefully making her way up the stairs. The blood was not in a simple single

85

trail, but splattered here and there. As she reached the landing at the top of the stairs, the puddle grew thicker and darker.

"A little over an hour I guess."

"Anything worthwhile?"

"Not that I could find. There *is* a huge difference here, though—so different that I at first thought this murder was not related to the others. The victim's name is Monica Knight. She's a pretty big-time local lawyer. She also happens to be single. She was married for less than six months but her husband had an affair and left her. That was about twelve years ago, from what I'm being told."

"So not a couple this time?"

"That's right," DeMarco said.

Kate reached the landing and looked down to the body. She was lying on her back, staring up at the ceiling with wide eyes. She had been stabbed multiple times, with most of the attention given to her stomach. One grisly wound etched across her neck and that was where most of the blood seemed to have come from.

"So, what makes it connect to the other murders?" Kate asked.

DeMarco held up a plastic evidence baggie. There was yet another piece of the blanket inside of it. "It was rough," she said. "It was shoved down her throat just like the others. The corner of it was sticking out of the wound in her throat. It had been shoved down in there so hard that one of her front teeth was loose."

"Any connection to the other victims?"

"Nothing apparent. That's what Palmetto is checking for us right now. He's tried reaching out to the ex-husband to warn him that he might be in danger but so far there's been no word."

Kate nodded and hunkered down into a squatting position. She looked closely at the victim's face and frowned. Monica Knight was very pretty, aside from all the blood. It was apparent that she took good care of her blonde hair and her complexion. But Kate also noted that Monica's beauty might come from another factor altogether.

"Hold on. Do we know how old she is?"

DeMarco scanned through some notes she had taken on her phone and said: "Thirty-nine."

"So she's at least ten to fifteen years younger than the other victims," Kate pointed out. "*And* single."

"Yeah, that seemed weird to me, too," DeMarco said. "The piece of fabric in her throat directly ties her to the other victims but that's where the connection ends."

So that eliminates the field of thought that the killer is only targeting couples, Kate thought. *It'll be interesting to see what we find out about the ex-husband.*

She took a closer look at the victim. Based on the trail of blood that led upstairs, there had apparently been some kind of a struggle or a chase. While it seemed odd at first glance that Monica Knight would have chosen to try running upstairs to escape, Kate had seen similar scenarios multiple times over the course of her career. Sometimes the victim had a gun upstairs and chose to try to get to it in order to defend themselves. Other times, the killer blocked the doorway and the victim chose to run upstairs to lock themselves in a bedroom or bathroom—which, in the grand scheme of things—was a pretty good method. In the age of cell phones, it worked more times than not.

Looking over the body, Kate counted at least seven stab wounds in the stomach but it was hard to tell. They were all so close to one another that the area started to look like nothing more than a mess of flesh, cloth from her shirt, and blood. The closeness of the wounds spoke of quick movements, the killer working like a machine. But the one along the throat was not as exact or neat as the others. There was tearing in the flesh as well as slicing. That cut had been done with extreme force, likely out of a deranged anger that was apparently not behind the stab wounds they had seen out of him so far.

As Kate looked Monica Knight's body over, DeMarco's phone rang. She answered it and spoke in a quick and efficient manner. Kate was impressed. DeMarco was able to cut straight to the point without coming off like a bitch or as if she did not care at all about the person on the other end of the line. Kate knew full well just how difficult that was to do.

"Hey, you got something?" DeMarco said as she answered the phone. Her eyes wandered as she listened to the person on the other end. "And someone actually spoke with him? Yeah? Okay...and would he be okay if I called as well? Great. Thanks."

She hung up without a goodbye and looked at Kate. "That was Palmetto," DeMarco said. "Someone on the police force got in touch with Knight's ex-husband. He's alive and well in Nashville, Tennessee. When he was told that his wife had been killed, he was quiet but didn't seem to care too much. But he managed to answer some questions satisfactorily."

"We should still maybe reach out to him when the dust has settled. I don't think it would be necessary to bring him here, but still…"

"Unless there's reason to believe he did it. And if he lives in Nashville and is there *right now,* that basically rules him out. Monica Knight hasn't been dead for much more than eight hours."

Downstairs, someone knocked on the door. "Agents? We good to come in?"

DeMarco nodded at Kate. "Forensics. I sent them packing for a little while when I knew for sure you were on the way."

Kate smiled. DeMarco had been by herself on the case for less than a day but was already running things as if it had been solely hers from the start. She was able to adapt and had the ability to make people respect her from the get-go; again, Kate knew how difficult this could be for a young, attractive woman as she had lived through it herself.

"Yeah, I think we're good here," Kate said to the man at the door below them. She took one final look back at the body, taking a mental picture.

She and DeMarco walked down the stairs as two more members of the forensics team walked into the house. They all passed one another with polite waves as Kate and DeMarco stepped out onto the porch.

"Who discovered the body?" Kate asked.

"Her boyfriend. They've been dating for about a year. His story checked out right away. He was on a plane, touching down in Raleigh, North Carolina, right around the time it's believed she was killed. I already had the flight logs checked and it's all legit."

"Did he name anyone who might have had a beef with her?"

"Well, she was a lawyer. So really, there's no shortage of people that might have *something* against her. But he was at a loss. Couldn't come up with anyone who might have wanted her dead."

"Who is Palmetto going to speak with today?" Kate asked.

"Two of her most recent clients. One was wrongly accused of abuse, or so the story goes. Seems it might be worth at least looking into and besides, Palmetto says he knows the defendant pretty well."

"We know where her parents live?"

"In Charlottesville, which is about an hour and a half away from here. I have them on the list of people to speak with. You think it's worth a visit?"

"I do. It goes back to the blanket. Something about including those scraps—shoving it down their throats—it seems personal in a weird way. I think if we get any leads at all on this, it's going to be from people who knew the victims intimately. More than just a boyfriend of one year or a cheating ex-husband."

And yet again, something she'd said to the assembled team in DC for the child abduction case repeated in her head: *Maybe it was right there in front of you the entire time but it looked so mundane and ordinary that you looked past it.*

"Yeah, that sounds legit," DeMarco said. "I know you just got off of the road and—"

Again, she was interrupted by her phone. She looked at it and said: "Palmetto again." She answered it with her same authoritative yet somehow warm tone. "Something else?"

Kate listened to one side of the conversation for about twenty seconds before DeMarco hung up. "Got something?" Kate asked.

"No. But it turns out we won't have to go to Charlottesville. Her parents are coming to Roanoke to stay with Monica's best friend while they plan for the funeral. They're asking to speak to whoever is in charge of her daughter's murder investigation right away."

"I suppose that would be us," Kate said. She looked back to the home of Monica Knight. There was a skeptical look on her face, as if she thought the house might be keeping a secret from them.

I'm missing something, Kate thought, growing more and more frustrated. *But what?*

Maybe speaking to Knight's parents would push her closer to discovering what it was. Or maybe, just maybe, they were dealing with a killer just crafty enough to leave no trace. Of course, she knew that even the type of mindset that set a killer toward a super-obsessive and neat crime scene could be a clue in and of itself.

Maybe that's where I need to look, Kate thought. *Maybe...*

"Agent Wise?" DeMarco asked. "You okay?"

"Yeah. Just trailing off with my thoughts," she said. She headed for the car, knowing the house would not give up any secrets it might have. Instead, she was going to have to dig them up herself...and that just happened to be something she was very good at.

CHAPTER EIGHTEEN

While the parents of Monica Knight gathered their bearings and took care of all of the necessities once they arrived in Roanoke, Kate sat in the conference room she and DeMarco had been given at the Roanoke Police Department. She read through every available file and form the PD had on the Langleys and the Nashes while roughly a dozen pages were being printed out concerning Monica Knight.

She was thinking of the Frank Costello case—of the YMCA in particular. And that got her to thinking about this unidentified partner that could very well be at work, leaving little inconspicuous clues behind in the form of empty nut wrappers and spilled snacks. What was her spilled snack here? What was right in front of her but going unseen?

DeMarco entered the room with the Knight files and handed Kate a copy. They looked through the files together, bouncing findings and ideas off of one another.

"Her college transcripts show that she had originally gone to school to study psychology," DeMarco said. "Namely early child development. Seems sort of creepy when you think of the blanket we're been finding traces of in the victims' throats."

"That *does* seem ominous," Kate said. "But what do you make of the two different requests to have fingerprints taken voluntarily, all within the last five years?"

DeMarco flipped through her pages until she came to this information. "That does seem strange. One of the requests is linked to an additional information request that she also sent to the Department of Social Services."

Kate hung on to that bit of information, sensing that there was something else there, something that could maybe tie it all together. But there was one thing missing—something she could not yet place.

Something in the Langley file...something similar...

She started to reach for the Langley file when there was a knock at the door. One of the deputies poked his head in, a frown on his face. "The parents of Monica Knight are here. Should I send them   in?"

"Yes," Kate said. "Give us two minutes, please."

The deputy nodded and the moment he was gone, Kate quickly thumbed through the Langley file. It didn't take her too long to find what she was looking for.

"There's a fingerprint request here for the Langleys, too," she said. She tapped at a carbon copy of the fingerprints of Scott and Bethany Langley. "Right here. They had to be fingerprinted when they were going through the process to be approved as foster parents."

"Maybe that's why Monica Knight needed to get fingerprinted?" DeMarco suggested. "It would certainly align with the ties to an information request to DSS."

Kate pondered this for a moment as she gathered up the files in front of her. The last thing she wanted was for a set of grieving parents to come in and see the life of their dead daughter crudely summed up in a series of pages. DeMarco followed suit and stuffed all of the paperwork into her laptop bag.

"Have you had to actively speak with grieving parents before?" Kate asked.

"A few times," she said. "You never really get used to it, though. I mean, when I was working Violent Crimes, there were other agents that did that sort of thing. Agents with a knack for grief psychology. Makes me wonder how doctors manage to do it all the time."

There was another knock at the door. This time when it opened, the same sad-looking deputy led an older couple into the room— Monica Knight's parents. Kate thought the mother might normally look rather young for her age but the act of furiously crying over the unexpected death of a child had taken its toll on her. She looked around the room wildly, as if untrusting of everything.

As for the father, he was a tall gentleman who looked like he was sleepwalking. The redness around their eyes made it clear that they had spent the better part of the last several hours crying over their child. But Kate could also see determination in the father's face; he was determined to be as strong as possible through all of this for his wife.

"This is Dean and Gloria Knight," the deputy said. "With all due respect, Agents, they want to help in any way they can but they also have family local to the area they'd like to get back to as soon as they can."

"We'll be as quick as we can," Kate said. "Thank you, Deputy."

The deputy left, leaving the room in silence. Kate had been down this road a million times and had learned not to dwell too much on the recent loss. It was often best to cut right to the chase, not to dwell on the murders but to start looking for solutions. It not only eliminated the chance of one of the parents breaking down, but it also made them feel assured that they would have answers soon.

"I understand your need to get back to your family as soon as possible," Kate said. "So we'll get right to it. We're looking for a connection between what has happened to your daughter and four other people in the area within the last four days. Up until Monica, we were under the assumption that it was just couples. And there are no direct links between the victims. So we were hoping you might be able to provide us with some insight. Any people that might be upset with Monica or anything she might have mentioned to you recently that threw up a red flag."

"She never really spoke about the negative aspects of her work," Dean Knight said. "But we've been asking ourselves the same thing. With her job, there would be far too many people that might have something against her, right?"

"The local PD is looking into it right now," DeMarco said. "And if no immediate answers are found, we'll also get bureau resources on it. For now, though, we're trying to concentrate on areas that might not be so obvious—things that may make your daughter similar to the others."

"That's right," Kate said. "We know that she was married at one time. And she had no children, correct?"

"That's right," Gloria Knight said. "In fact, I've always believed that's one of the reasons her no good husband ran out on her. Monica *always* wanted kids. She used to joke about how she wanted to start trying to get pregnant as soon as her honeymoon. But her husband was never on the same wavelength."

"She was going to adopt for a while," Dean said. "But I think she started to get far too involved in her career."

"Did she ever *actually* adopt?" Kate asked, starting to feel a thread picking up and knitting itself into the narrative.

"No," Gloria said. "She *did* foster for a while. Just short-terms thing here and there, though."

"How long did she do that?" Kate asked, thinking about those fingerprint requests and DSS paperwork.

"About three or four years, I suppose," Gloria said.

Kate knew what she wanted to do next but measured the possible outcome for a moment. She and DeMarco shared a glance, both aware that they had perhaps stumbled upon something with the foster parent connection. The Langleys, after all, had served as foster parents as well. That still left the Nashes unconnected from it all, but at least it felt like they were getting *somewhere.*

"I'd like to show you something," Kate said. She took the scrap of blanket that she had been holding onto ever since they had first met Palmetto. She did not set it on the table, but held on to it in the event that it *did* look familiar to the Knights. If they responded harshly, she wanted to be able to hide it away as soon as possible.

But she could tell right away that it meant nothing to them. Gloria Knight stared at the scrap of fabric so hard that Kate was pretty sure she was trying to make herself find some connection—anything to find answers about her daughter's death. But after several seconds, she shook her head.

"No. Should it?"

"We don't know," DeMarco said. "But scraps similar to this have been found at all of the crime scenes. So far, it seems to be the only stable connection."

"As for now," Kate said, "I believe that's really all we need. We'll let you get back to your family, but please, if you think of anything—no matter how small or insignificant it may seem—please contact us."

"We will," Dean said as he slowly got up. He took Gloria by the arm and they walked slowly together toward the door. Gloria gave one hopeful look back and said, "Please find out who did this."

She made her way through the door like a woman in a dream. The moment the doors were closed, DeMarco took the files and papers back out on the three different crime scenes.

"There's nothing in the Nashes' history dealing with foster care in any way, shape, or form," she said.

"Well, maybe it's something else, some other connection," Kate said. "What about DSS? Any dealings between the Nashes and the Department of Social Services?"

"I don't think so," DeMarco said. "But I can get someone on the PD to look into it."

"That might be our best bet for now," Kate said.

DeMarco looked at her skeptically and smiled thinly. "Are you sure about that? You look like you're hooked on some other thought."

Kate nodded, not denying it. She was both impressed and a little uneasy that DeMarco already knew her tics and mannerisms so well.

"I'm choosing to focus on the painfully obvious," she said. "We can't find any one thing that connects all of the victims so far. But the killer himself is connecting them for us."

"With the scraps of blanket," DeMarco said.

"Exactly. It's like his calling card. And if it's a children's blanket, maybe it's a relic from his childhood."

"You think the killer knew this victims when he was a kid?"

"Possibly," Kate said.

She'd worked with enough cases stemming from a killer's childhood trauma in the past to know that she was no expert in the field. The good news for Kate, though, was that her career had pointed her in the direction of such experts. And it seemed like it was pointing her that way once again.

Only, with a killer still at large and a set of grieving parents having just left their presence less than two minutes ago, it seemed to be less of a *pointing* and more of an urgent push.

"How's the Internet in this building?" Kate asked.

"Decent. Why?"

"Open up Skype on your laptop," Kate said. "I need to make a call."

CHAPTER NINETEEN

Kate had not expected Dr. Henrietta Yates to answer her Skype call right away. Kate had worked closely with Yates more than twenty times over the course of her career and knew that she was one of the most prominent psychologists in the field of early child development and behaviors. If the blanket held more meaning than Kate was able to decipher, Yates would be able to help.

Kate placed a call to Dr. Yates's office and, after a few back and forth calls with her receptionist, was able to schedule an impromptu face-to-face via DeMarco's laptop. In the time that passed, she took a picture of the ragged fragment of blanket and emailed it to Yates. DeMarco took the opportunity to put in an urgent request with the Records department.

When Yates's face came onto the screen, she was quickly brushing her hair aside with one hand and sipping from a cup of tea with the other. It was apparent that she was in the midst of a busy day, making Kate feel guilty for interrupting her.

"Agent Wise," Dr. Yates said. "It's great to hear from you. It's been what? At least two years, right?"

"Probably more," Kate said.

"I heard through the grapevine that you had retired."

"Yeah, that didn't work out."

"Yeah, I was surprised," Yates said. "The mere idea of retirement doesn't seem to even make sense when I think of you."

"Dr. Yates, I know you're a busy woman and your receptionist told me you had to push some things back to arrange this call. I appreciate that and we will make this as quick as possible."

"No worries," Yates said, though it was clear that there were at least *some* worries. It was apparent she was preoccupied with her own work. "What can I do for you, Agent Wise?"

"I sent you a picture a few minutes ago," Kate said. "It's a torn piece of a blanket. That fragment as well as two others have recently been found at murder scenes. To this point, it's the only evidence that connects the victims. And it's purposefully being left behind by the killer. I was thinking it might have something to do with his childhood…maybe a keepsake or something."

"That's a safe assumption," Yates said. "How are you finding them? Are they carefully set aside or placed on the bodies?"

"They're being shoved down the throats of the victims. Forensics seems to think it's done *after* the murder."

"Well that *does* paint a better picture. You know as well as I do that anything so tangible that is left behind is being left behind for a reason—if not to draw you closer to finding him, then to appease some nostalgic or self-obsessed part of himself. If this blanket *is* from his childhood, then I'd assume the victims are also somehow tied to his childhood. Or at least the killer would think so. Another thing to consider is the throat the fabric was put into."

"I don't follow you."

"I mean, were the victims male or female?"

"That's another interesting thing," Kate said. "The first murders were couples. Two of them. The third scene was a single woman. At the two scenes with the couples, the fabric was—"

"—in the throat of the women, right?" Yates asked.

"Yes, that's right," Kate said, unable to bite back a smile at Yates's intuition.

"Agent Wise, I'd bet just about everything I have on the fact that these murders are based on some sort of perceived wrongdoing from the killer. He likely wasn't nurtured much as a child or maybe he was and he just grew up to have a skewed sense of what nurturing and security meant to him. And going back to the blanket…killers will often leave something behind that is connected to a specific incident or time in their life that deeply affected them."

"So the tendency towards couples and placing the fabric in the throats of the mothers…you think it's a yearning for a family?"

"Perhaps," Yates said. "But this would be a killer already cemented in a deep state of psychosis. If anything, singling the women out in such a way makes me think he's got some sort of trauma in his past with a mother figure. Blankets in a child's hands are meant to be comforting. And if you look at the mother and father interplay, it's typically the mothers that are viewed as the more comforting."

The Langleys and Monica Knight were foster parents, Kate thought. *I bet if we start looking at lists of kids they fostered, we'll see the killer's name on those lists.*

As if Yates had also already picked up on a similar train of thought, she went on. "Now, I can't be sure, but this looks like it might be fabric from some sort of a child's blanket. Can you confirm that?"

"Basically. I've even spoken the company that likely manufactured it."

As she said this, someone knocked on the conference room door. DeMarco answered it as Yates responded. Kate watched as an officer handed DeMarco a small stack of papers.

"The fact that blankets are often seen as security objects even up into the teen years speaks volumes," Yates said. This killer is bringing something usually seen as something used for comfort into murder scenes. What about the murders themselves? Quick and precise or violent?"

"Violent."

DeMarco was looking over the papers that had just been delivered to her. Slowly, a dawning excitement started to bloom over her face.

On the laptop screen, Yates was nodding her head. "Yes, I'd go so far as to say that this is starting to look like a textbook case of a killer that is blaming something traumatic from his childhood on parents. Maybe parents he did not have."

"Yes, we think there might be a parent element to it," Kate said. "And with that, Doctor Yates, I'm happy to say you can get back to your job. You've given what was a rather lame lead some very strong legs to stand on for right now."

"Good to hear," Dr. Yates said. "Glad to help. And, might I add, it's good to see you working again. Just couldn't stay away, could you?"

"Something like that," Kate said with a smile. "Thanks again, Doctor."

With that, Kate ended the call. She instantly looked over to DeMarco as she still looked through the papers the officer had given her.

"What have you got?" Kate asked.

"Just a bit more information on the Nashes," she said. She slid a Xeroxed sheet over to Kate and added, "It appears that the Nashes also set up an appointment to get fingerprinted at some point in the past. And it appears that it had to do with this."

She slid another sheet over to Kate. Kate looked them over and knew instantly where this was headed. She saw a copy of the Nashes' fingerprints, taken in 2007. With the prints were the typical form requests for a background check. Within the background check information, there was also a request for the information from the Department of Social Services.

The second sheet was fresher; Kate could still feel the slight warmth of it having just come out of a printer. There was a scrawled message at the top, blurred from a recent copy of it being made that read: *Hope this is what you were looking for! – Ruby.*

Beneath that scripted message, there was a very simple application form for an organization called Family Friends and Services. It had been filled out by Toni Nash and signed by both Toni and Derrick Nash. The questions on the application were all family or child related—all questions that pointed back to their foster care connection. *How many children have you raised? Why are you interested in caring for children in emergency situations? Do you have ample room within your home to care for a child?*

There were more questions like this, all given appropriate and well-thought-out answers by Toni Nash.

"Have you ever heard of this Family Friends and Services?" DeMarco asked.

"Nope. It's new to me. Sounds a lot like foster care. But the term *foster care* is never used on this application."

"So maybe we pay our new friend Ruby a visit," DeMarco said, pointing to the name at the top of the application.

They got up together, working like a well-oiled machine. It made Kate wonder, if only briefly, what it might have been like to work with DeMarco if she, Kate, were about twenty years younger. They had a connection established between them already that most paired agents could only hope to have after years of working together.

As they left the station, headed for the offices of Family Friends and Services, Kate was once again reminded why she loved this job. It was more than just the thrill of the hunt or putting puzzle pieces together as a case started to come into focus—it was the sense of partnership and camaraderie, too.

It made the discovery of a potential lead all the more exciting. And it also made Kate feel a bit more confident and secure as the endgame slowly came into view.

CHAPTER TWENTY

The central office at Family Friends and Services was a large, brightly lit space. Three of the walls were adorned with canvas prints of smiling children's faces. The fourth wall was filled with a map of the Roanoke area and a large whiteboard adorned with names and dates. Kate and DeMarco sat on one side of a large conference table while the red-headed woman in her early fifties sat down across from them with a mug of coffee. This was Ruby Hendricks, the Director of Operations for Family Friends and Services. She looked bright-eyed and happy but Kate could see nervousness ticking along at the corners of her mouth as well.

"Ms. Hendricks, thank you for meeting with us on such short notice," Kate said.

"Of course. With my position with FFS, I'm rarely out of the office. What is it, exactly, that I can help you with? Is it about the Nashes?"

"You've already heard about them?" DeMarco asked.

"Yes. Cami Nash let me know about it."

"So you knew the Nashes well?" Kate asked.

"Not on a very personal level, but I knew them enough to consider them friends," Ruby said. "I saw them here in the office a few times and they also attended most of our fundraising events."

"Well, as it turns out, we *are* here to ask about the Nashes," Kate said. "We learned today that they were part of Family Friends and Services. However, we really have no idea what you do here."

"Oh," Ruby said, seemingly delighted that she was fielding such an easy question. "Well, I don't know if you are aware of this or not, but the area of Central Virginia has a fairly large foster parent problem. There simply aren't enough people fostering to cover the need for children that are looking for safe homes. The ratio is something like one potential foster home per eighteen kids. What we here at FFS do is step in as a temporary alternate. We consider ourselves a prevention from foster care, actually."

"Is that really a necessary step?" Kate asked.

"Oh yes. Don't get me wrong…there is nothing at all wrong with foster care. I myself am foster approved. But many people abuse the system. And because it is state run, the wait times for paperwork and approvals can take forever. We try to sidestep all of that, and even DSS is starting to realize the need for a service like ours. I can give you an example, actually. Two days ago, we were contacted by DSS. A mother had given birth to her baby and it was discovered in the hospital that the baby was born substance exposed. The mother had done drugs up into the sixth month of pregnancy. Social services removed the baby from the mother but the mother did not want her child getting lost in the foster care system. Instead, she signed the baby over to us and the child is now in the care of one of our Family Friends and Services families. It saves the state the money and hustle of working up an emergency foster situation and gives the mother ample time to clean herself up and get back on her feet. When she *is* a fit mother, we will return her child to her but only after DSS has deemed her suitable."

"And this is all legal?" DeMarco asked.

"Of course. There are actually organizations like this spread out over the country but we don't get much press. Courts only consider cases a so-called victory in a lot of cases if endangered children are placed into foster care because *foster* care is a well-known term. But what we do is essentially the same, only we get no monthly stipend check."

"It's all volunteer?" DeMarco asked.

"Correct. Most of our families are heavily involved in churches or other child care organizations."

"Do the families need to be foster approved?" Kate asked.

"No. And that's another audience we appeal to. Many parents—or former parents, for that matter—don't want to be foster parents but they *do* have a heart for children in need."

"And I assume the Nashes were on your list of participating families?" Kate asked.

"Yes, they were. They had been with us for about ten years or so, I'd guess. Maybe longer. I can pull the records for you, if you like."

"That would be great," Kate said.

"One moment, then," Ruby said as she got up and headed for the door.

When she closed the door behind her, Kate said: "So that explains why the Nashes didn't come up on any foster parent databases."

"And while it's not foster care per se, I think involvement in Family Friends and Services would be close enough—close enough to establish a solid connection between all three families, anyway."

"So now the trick is to see if there are any children that these three families had in common," Kate said. "Was there one single child that all three families kept at some point? And that could lead us straight to the killer."

Both women mulled over this for a moment. It was an exciting thought, but part of Kate thought that it felt just a tad too easy.

Ruby returned two minutes later with a thin binder. The name NASH was typed down the spine. She opened the binder up and turned it so that it was facing Kate and DeMarco.

"Derrick and Toni Nash became part of the Family Friends and Services family in 2007," Ruby said. "They hosted their first child later that year, through Christmas, I believe. Over the last twelve years or so, they've hosted fourteen children, ages six months to fourteen."

"And to become a member of your organization, I assume they had to pass background checks?" DeMarco asked.

"Absolutely. Honestly, anyone applying for FFS has to pretty much undergo the same things as someone working towards becoming a foster parent. The only difference is that I believe with foster care, there are classes you have to take and pass."

"Do you keep a list of the names of the children each family hosts?" Kate asked.

"We do," Ruby said, looking rather uncomfortable. "But...well, as FBI agents, I'm sure you understand that I can't very well just hand that kind of information over to you. I'd love to...really, I would. I'm sick over what happened to the Nashes. But we can't give that information out. What I *can* do is direct you to one of the case workers over at Social Services that should be able to get you the entire list."

Kate didn't bother pushing the issue. She knew Ruby was right and while it would slow them down a bit, she understood the safety measures of such a process. "We'd greatly appreciate the number of whichever case worker you feel would act the most urgently on this."

"Of course," Ruby said, scrolling through her phone in search of the contact information.

"Also," Kate said, "with an organization like this, I would assume you see a lot of kids that come through here dealing with varied forms of trauma. Would that be accurate?"

"Yes, unfortunately."

"Is there a local therapist you work with to help with those sorts of cases?"

"Yes, actually. As a matter of fact, she's located just right down the street."

"In that case, thank you for your time," Kate said.

Ruby nodded and grabbed a pen from the table. She jotted down the information of the DSS worker and handed it to DeMarco.

"I mean this when I say it," Ruby said. "Please let me know if there is anything else I can do to help. The Nashes were among the best people I ever met—nice, charitable, and kind. They didn't deserve this."

Kate nodded, keeping in the comment that sprang up in her mind. *That might be so,* she thought. *But someone thought they did deserve it. And someone with that kind of skewed mentality might be much more dangerous than we could have ever thought.*

***

Knowing the rigid process that state judiciary systems put in place to protect the private information of citizens, Kate knew that a direct call to the Department of Social Services would do her no good. They'd ask to speak to her supervisor and they'd work the details out with them. So instead of calling DSS directly, Kate placed a call to Duran. She gave him the information of Ruby's DSS contact and let him know what they were looking for. He ended the call with the promise that he'd get back to her in fifteen minutes with the names of all of the children who had ever been cared for by the Nashes, the Langleys, and Monica Knight.

That little errand allowed Kate and DeMarco enough time to visit the office of the Family Friends and Services' therapist at the other end of the street. Ruby had handed Kate a business card as they had left FFS with the name of Danielle Ethridge and the office address. The same name was on the glass door of the office in white vinyl letters.

Inside, a receptionist sat at a desk, typing something into a laptop. It was a small space, probably a private practice of some sort. The place was well decorated and very homey, reminding Kate of the offices at Family Friends and Services. The receptionist looked up and smiled as they entered.

"Hello, ladies," she said a little too cheerfully. "Can I help you?"

As they approached the desk, Kate showed her ID, as did DeMarco. As they went through their introductions, the woman's good cheer seemed to evaporate. And when they explained that they were there to speak with Dr. Ethridge concerning a rather time-sensitive case, she looked downright scared.

"Of course, of course," the receptionist said. "Unfortunately, Dr. Ethridge is with a patient right now. But I can let her know you are here just as soon as the session is over. It shouldn't be long. Maybe another fifteen minutes."

"Thank you," Kate said. They walked over to a small seating area and when she sat down, the very feel of inactivity made Kate feel like the case was indeed coming together. She'd garnered something of an instinct based on her emotions; when she was at a standstill in a case but it wasn't leading anywhere, she tended to get anxious. On the other hand, as she and DeMarco sat in the waiting area, she felt at peace—as if they were close enough to the end of this thing that they did not have to rush.

Seven minutes into their wait, they each got a text from Duran through a group text. **Emailing a list of names from DSS within 5 mins.**

"That should wrap it up, right?" DeMarco asked. "If we can find one name on these lists that stayed with the Nashes, the Langleys, and Monica Knight, that will be the smoking gun, right?"

"It feels that way," Kate said. "On the other hand, it could also do nothing more than shoot down a lead." Honestly, she did not feel this way but she didn't want to show DeMarco, a younger and still moldable agent, that it was okay to rest on your laurels and simply assume that things were going well.

Kate kept an eye on her phone and when she got the notification that she had a new mail, she opened it right away. Strangely, she felt a stirring of compassion when she saw the lists. The Nashes alone had hosted six children through Family Friends and Services. The Langleys had cared for six, while Monica Knight had housed four foster kids. It was heartwarming to know that there were people in the world who still cared for orphans and troubled children in such a way. It made her think of Michelle and how she would be fortunate to grow up in a home where she would always be loved.

There was a note at the bottom of the lists. It read: *Not a complete list. Some children had their names changed. Some parents had them removed once they resumed care. Others were removed from all lists at their own request after turning eighteen years of age.*

"I see two in common right away," DeMarco said, looking at her own mail.

Kate spotted that, too. And while she hated to instantly eliminate so many other names from the list, it simply made more sense to go with the children whom all of the victims had in common. Seeing these two names, she *did* start to feel a slight bit of anxiousness slipping into her mind.

"Agents?"

They looked up and saw a middle-aged woman in glasses approaching them. Like the receptionist, she smiled widely. She wore a pair of glasses that made her eyes appear very bright.

Kate stood up and shook the woman's hand. DeMarco followed suit.

"Thanks for meeting with us," Kate said. "As I told your receptionist, it's a time-sensitive matter."

"Yes, and I got a text from Ruby that told me you were coming as well. So come on back, Agents, and let me see if I can help."

***

Kate and DeMarco sat on the opposite side of Dr. Ethridge as she slowly lowered herself into the chair behind her desk. "Do you mind if I ask if this matter is about the Langleys and the Nashes?" she asked.

"It is," Kate said, surprised that she knew about one other family that Ruby at Family Friends had not known about. "And if I'm going to be blunt and expect your full cooperation, I suppose I can also tell you that as of this morning, another woman has been killed—Monica Knight."

"Oh my God," she said. "I never really knew her, but heard of her. She wasn't with FSS, correct?"

"Not that we know of," Kate said. "Just foster care."

"We're here," DeMarco said, "because so far the only link we can find between the victims is the fact that they were all connected through the foster system in one way or the other, although we understand the Nashes weren't foster parents, but involved in Family Friends and Services."

"And while we can't go into detail just yet," Kate said, "the killer has been leaving little clues behind that indicate he may have some sort of trauma from his childhood that is still tormenting him."

"I'll help in whatever capacity I can," Ethridge said, "but surely you understand that there will be areas where my hands are tied when it comes to doctor-patient confidentiality."

"Yes," Kate said, fully expecting this. "But I don't think you'll have to divulge too much." She slid her phone over to Ethridge and showed her the list of names. "As you'll see, there are two names that the victims have in common. Two children."

"Yes, I was aware of at least one child that both the Nashes and the Langleys had seen. I don't know if Ruby told you, but I also see quite a few children from DSS cases, particularly after the kids have been moved into foster care. I don't get them all, but I do get many of them."

"So these two children," DeMarco said. "Do the names ring bells? Or, more importantly, do they raise any red flags?"

"Well, Renee Pearson was a handful," Ethridge said, pointing to a name on the list. "I had no idea she had ended up with Monica Knight, though. It might have been just a respite situation where care was only needed for a day or so. Anyway, Renee was always looking for an argument. She'd lash out at people, hitting them in the hopes of getting into a fight. In her first foster home, she was caught holding a pillow over the face of the family's three-year-old son while he slept. The kid was okay, thankfully, but the trouble that Renee got into didn't seem to bother her at all."

"So you'd say she had a tendency toward violence?" Kate asked.

"Yes, that's a safe bet. But...this was nearly...God, almost twelve years ago the last time I saw her. She found a home that sort of fit. Last I heard—and it's been a while—she had gone to college."

"Do you know if she still lives around here?" DeMarco asked.

"Pretty sure. If you'll check with my receptionist on the way out, she might have a current address that we use for Christmas cards and the like."

"Anyone else in that trio stand out?" Kate asked.

Ethridge nodded. "Yeah. Robert Traylor. He was one of those young boys that just...I hate to say it, but you could see the hate in his eyes sometimes. Abandoned as a baby, sexually abused by a foster father when he was four. Robert was cutting himself when he was nine or so—and that was right around the time his uncle finally took him in. That helped for a while from what I can remember, but he got taken in by the cops for the first time when he was eleven or twelve."

"What for?" DeMarco asked.

"Beating up a homeless man. Smashed a liquor bottle right over his head."

"Did he ever threaten you?" Kate asked.

"Oh yeah, almost weekly. He threatened to break into my house and rape me. Pretty harsh words coming from a thirteen-year-old."

"At the risk of jumping to conclusions, do you think he'd be capable of murder?"

Ethridge thought about this for a moment. She steepled her fingers together as she thought, clearly not wanting to take the conversation where it was headed. "I can clearly remember putting notes like *self-harm* and *suicidal thoughts and tendencies* into his evaluations. And that was pretty much over the entire time I saw him as a patient. I suppose he'd be in his late twenties now. Maybe early thirties. And while I am a huge proponent of thinking anyone can change, I just…well, I find it hard to think that he could have changed *that* much."

"Have you seen or heard from him since you last met with him professionally?" DeMarco asked.

"No. And that's been nearly nine years ago."

Kate nodded and got to her feet. As far as she was concerned, they had what they needed. "Well, thanks for your time—again, we certainly appreciate it."

"Agent Wise…do you mind me asking what the killer is leaving behind? You said there were clues he was leaving behind."

"Fragments of what appear to be an old blanket."

"Like a security blanket?"

"That's the hunch I'm going with. Why do you ask?"

Ethridge thought for a moment before answering: "That's a pretty sentimental object." Kate waited for something else, but Ethridge looked lost in thought.

Kate gave a final nod of appreciation and then left the office.

On the way down the hall, DeMarco pulled out her phone. "I doubt someone like Robert Traylor is on the Christmas card list," she said. "I'll put in an information request on his current residence."

"And if Renee Pearson is local, let's pay her a visit, too," Kate said. "Maybe she can offer some insight into how being bounced around from home to home can alter a kid's thinking."

But even while they were making these plans, the last thing Ethridge said remained stuck in her head. It slowly started to glow, as if it might have some meaning to it, some clue to help them break the case.

That's a pretty sentimental object, Ethridge had said of the blanket.

It was a notion that Kate had felt ever since the beginning, but she could not tease out the meaning of it just yet.

Maybe when they encountered Robert Traylor, he'd be able to tell them himself—from the confines of an interrogation room.

CHAPTER TWENTY ONE

Renee Pearson—now Renee Matthews after getting married three years ago—lived just outside of Roanoke, in a neighborhood nestled in a valley that gave a breathtaking view of the mountains. Seeing the neighborhood was, to Kate, an exercise in not pre-judging people based on their history. The neighborhood was a gated community, with houses that would easily go for seven to eight hundred thousand in this part of the country. Dusk was only an hour or so away, the evening light painting the neighborhood in rich colors that seemed to add to the value of the place.

Just as Kate was parking along the curb in front of Renee Matthews's house, DeMarco's phone rang. She answered it right away. Kate continued to admire the neighborhood from behind the wheel as she listened to DeMarco's side of the phone conversation. She was off in less than a minute and although Kate had gotten the gist from DeMarco's end, her partner filled her in.

"So there appears to be no current residence for Robert Traylor," DeMarco said. "The last actual address on file for him was in Blacksburg, Virginia, and that was three years ago. The post office can confirm that he no longer lives there. The best we could get was the address of his uncle. They were apparently fairly tight at one point."

"He local?" Kate asked.

"Just outside of Blacksburg. About an hour and a half away."

"Maybe too late to visit tonight. We can call him when we leave here to see how cooperative he'll be."

They got out of the car and walked up to the porch. DeMarco knocked on the door and it was answered right away by a man carrying a toddler. The kid sucked on a bottle and looked at the agents skeptically.

"Can I help you?" the man asked.

"We're looking for Renee Matthews, formerly Renee Pearson," Kate said.

"That's my wife," he said. He then gave them a skeptical look that mirrored that of his son. "Can I ask who's visiting?"

"Agents Wise and DeMarco, with the FBI," Kate said, showing her ID. "We just need to ask her some questions about some people from her past."

"Ah," the husband said, as if it all made sense now. "Come on in. Renee is in the laundry room. I'll get her."

Mr. Pearson led them into the dining room and offered them both seats while he walked to the back of the house. Kate was glad to see that someone with a marred past had managed to do so well for themselves. Even if it was a case of marrying well, it was something to admire.

Moments later, a pretty woman dressed in a T-shirt and sweatpants came into the dining room. Her blonde hair was done up in a messy bun that made her look about ten years younger. Kate thought she could catch glimpses of the young girl who had once met with Dr. Ethridge.

"Renee?" Kate asked.

"Yeah, that's me," she said. "Chris said you were with the FBI?"

"That's right," DeMarco said, showing her badge.

"Is something wrong?" Renee asked.

"I don't know if you've heard about the Langleys and the Nashes yet," Kate said. "But they've recently been killed."

Renee nodded her head. "Yes. A friend of mine from in town called me. One day after the other, like a double play of terrible news."

"Had you remained close with them over the years?" Kate asked.

"I spoke with Toni Nash every now and then," Renee said. "She would occasionally call to tell me about Olivia being in college. I hadn't spoken to the Langleys in a while, though. They called on my birthday last year and I think that was the last time I spoke with them."

Kate did her best to deliver the next news softly. "What can you tell us about Monica Knight?" she asked.

"A nice enough lady. I stayed with her for about a week when I was fourteen or so and then for a weekend the year after that. She's such a sweet woman, but looking back, I think she was at war with which to give in to: her heart for kids or her career."

"Well, I hate to tell you that she's been killed, too," Kate said. "Sometime last night, we think."

Renee's hand went to her mouth and tears formed in her eyes.

"When did you speak to her last?" DeMarco asked.

"Oh, it's been years. I was married three years ago and she sent me a gift through Amazon. She never called. I invited her to the wedding, but she didn't come."

"How was your time with her when she hosted you?" Kate asked.

"Fine. Nothing special. We got along but nothing really ever clicked, you know? She was very kind and hospitable but there was never any real sense that she wanted to get to know me on a personal level."

"During your time with the Langleys, Nashes, and Monica Knight, did you happen to ever cross paths with a young man named Robert Traylor?"

Renee considered it for a moment before shaking her head. "It doesn't sound familiar. But then again, I was yanked around a lot for several years there."

"We spoke with Dr. Ethridge in Roanoke," DeMarco said. She smiled and added: "It looks like you got things turned around."

"I did," Renee said, wiping a tear away. "I met this college girl at one of the foster homes I was in and she was telling me how awesome college was and how she basically already had a job lined up when she graduated. I decided I'd give it a go. Did some community college to get my GPA up and then went to Virginia Tech. I graduated the same year Chris and I got married. I've been working with the Forestry Department ever since. I think it's a job that'll eventually lead us to West Virginia to live, but we're not quite sure yet."

"Now, just for the sake of us having to do our jobs," Kate said, "would you be able to prove your whereabouts every night for the past week or so?"

Alarmed, Renee sat up rigid in her seat. "Are you seriously suggesting that I—"

"I'm suggesting nothing," Kate said. "However, so far the only thing that these victims have in common is the fact that they were involved in foster care and child protection. And you were a common link among them all."

Renee looked pissed but it was also clear that she understood their approach. "I was here every night for the last week, with the exception of Thursday night. That's our date night. We have a sitter come so Chris and I can go out to dinner."

"And I'm sure that will all check out," DeMarco said apologetically. "Mrs. Matthews, you knew all five of these victims. Is there any reason at all you could think of for someone to want to hurt them? Was there maybe anything that linked them together somehow?"

"I honestly don't know," Renee said. "I can't think of anything. Then again, I was very self-absorbed and wrapped up in myself during that time in my life."

Kate got to her feet, a little regretful that they had driven out here for this brief and uneventful conversation. "Well, over the next day or so, we'd appreciate it if you could give it some thought. If you come up with anything, please let us know."

"Of   course."
With that, DeMarco left a business card on the dining room table as Renee walked them to the door.

"You know," Renee said, "foster care is a double-edged sword. For every great family, there's a shitty one. I heard about some pretty bad stories. But I find it hard to believe any of these families would have done something so bad to a child that would cause this."

"Did you ever meet a kid that was abused in the system?" Kate asked.

"A few girls here and there, yeah."

"And would you happen to know any of the names of those abusive families?"

"No…sorry."

"How about you?" DeMarco asked. "Did you ever experience it?"

"No. The Nashes and Langleys were the only actual *homes* I stayed in."

So there goes any hope of singling out the next family on the killer's list, Kate thought.

They thanked Renee one last time and headed back to the car. As Kate cranked the engine to life, DeMarco looked thoughtfully out the window.

"So if this killer *is* a former foster kid with connections to his victims, how can we know when he's done?"

"What do you mean?" Kate asked.

"What if he's like Renee? What if these were the only families he stayed with? What if he's killed them and has quit? He could have already gone into hiding."

"Then let's go find the bastard," Kate said and shifted the car into Drive.

CHAPTER TWENTY TWO

Despite the late hour, Kate was actually glad that the uncle of Robert Traylor agreed to meet with them. His only caveat was that they meet him at a bar in downtown Roanoke. So as the night wound closer to nine o'clock, Kate found herself driving back into Roanoke, following GPS directions to a bar called Shorty's Pub.

They found him at the back of the place, in a corner booth that looked like something that had been torn straight from an old noir movie. A pitcher of beer and a half-empty glass sat in front of him. He was vaguely watching one of the TVs behind the bar, squinting at the highlights on Sports Center.

"Mr. Traylor?" Kate asked as they approached the table.

He looked away from the television and to the two agents. His startled look made it clear that he probably wasn't expecting two women—although Kate was the one he talked to on the phone. An embarrassed look crossed his face, one that he turned toward the pitcher of beer and then back to them.

"Al Traylor," he said. "Nice to meet you. Want a drink?"

Kate would have loved a glass of white wine but she had never been one to drink on the job—not even after hours when she was away from DC.

"No thanks," she said. DeMarco shook her head as well. "Mr. Traylor, I'm Agent Wise and this is Agent DeMarco. As you were told on the phone, we were hoping to speak with you about a case we're working on."

Traylor nodded and sipped from his beer. The glass wasn't quite empty yet but he refilled it from the pitcher in front of him—which was, itself, about half-empty.

"You don't look very surprised," DeMarco said.

"Is it about my stupid fucking nephew?" he asked.

"It is, actually," Kate said. "What made you go there so quickly?"

"Because the boy is an accident waiting to happen. A fuck-up of massive proportions. I'm surprised I haven't been visited by the feds before now." He then chuckled and waved his hand at the glass and pitcher in front of him. "Like I have any room to speak. But, you know, he's the reason I drink so damned much."

Kate and DeMarco sat down on the other end of the booth. "Can you explain that, please?" Kate asked.

"Well, I guess you know he was bounced around in foster care for most of his childhood, right?" When the agents nodded, he nodded right back and then continued. "Well, I was a mess myself for a while. I drank a lot. Got fired from a few jobs because of it. Had three affairs on my wife before she wised up and left me. So yeah…I was a train wreck even before I met him. And then one day, I get this call from Social Services. They say they've got my nephew and they are looking for a home for him. Apparently, my idiot brother, God rest his miserable soul, skipped town and left his kid behind when he was just a baby—I didn't have a clue because we weren't in touch. He'd been bounced around in foster care until they finally found me. I didn't have him for very long, though, before he was put back in foster care."

"Why did they remove him from your care?" Kate asked.

Traylor pointed to the pint glass in front of him. "I didn't know they do surprise visits. Child Protective Services came by one evening to check on us and I was pretty drunk. Left him playing out in the front yard by himself."

"How old was he at this time?" DeMarco asked.

"Eight or nine. I don't really remember."

"And did he eventually get back into your care?"

"Yes," Traylor said. "I realized that I had wrecked my life, you know. So I cleaned up. Got *almost* sober. Got a steady job. I took the classes for foster care services and everything after I learned that he was just being passed around. There was a rumor that one of the families had been abusing him. So I asked for him back. I passed every class and course they threw at me and he seemed happy enough to be back with me. He lived with me for about a year before he ran away the first time. The cops brought him back three weeks later and he stayed with me again for a few months before he skipped out on me again."

"How was the relationship between the two of you?" Kate asked.

"Shitty at first. But we got to like one another, you know. We watched football on Sundays. Went fishing from time to time…which he hated, but he liked to be outdoors. I asked him, after that first time, why he ran away. He told me he got bored. I asked him where he went and he would never tell me. He got very shady about it."

"After he left the second time, was that the end of it?" Kate asked.

"Oh no. He showed up again when he was sixteen. Scrawny and long grungy hair. Had a girl with him this time. He asked if they could stay with me for a while and I said they could. I'd smell pot coming from his room from time to time. Heard loud sex noises, things like that. I had a talk with him about the girl having to find her own place and that did not go well. He blew up at me but he stayed, you know? He seemed different. Like…he knew how to use people. He was only with me this time for a safe place to stay. I knew that…but…"

He stopped here and took another gulp from his glass. He licked his lips and then continued. "They went out one night and I snooped through his stuff. I wanted to know what he into, where he had been, you know? And there was some dark stuff. Satanic stuff. Violent porn. Things like that. I confronted him about it because, quite frankly, some of the porn had some models that couldn't have been any older than fifteen or sixteen. Needless to say, he went nuts. Pulled a fucking knife on me. I think he would have actually stabbed me if I hadn't punched him first. He stormed out, told me to go to hell."

"Any idea where he went?" Kate asked.

"No. But, because I guess he thought I was a sucker, he came back on Christmas Eve two years after that. He was strung out on something. High as hell, you know? He asked if he could stay and I let him—but only through the New Year. He was doing coke in my house, smoking pot, bringing these fucking creepy people over to hang out, and God knows what else. I gave him until the middle of January to find a job. After he hadn't even tried, I sent him packing. And that's the last time I saw him."

"How long ago was that?" DeMarco asked.

"That's been about three years ago."

"Do you have any idea where we might find him?" Kate asked. "His last listed address is a dead end."

Traylor chuckled. "Oh, I bet it is. And his name probably wouldn't come up under any current address anyway. The moron changed his name. And I found *that* out when I got a letter in the mail last year. Said he had moved, changed his name, and was starting over. He asked for money in the letter—just to get back on his feet. I crumpled it up and threw it away. But yeah, I have his address…and his new name: Chester Black, and he lives in a trailer out in Whip Springs, back in the woods somewhere."

"You say he pulled a knife on you at one time," Kate said. "Do you think that was him acting out of anger or being high…or do you think that sort of reaction is just in his nature?"

"I don't follow you."

"Do you think he'd be capable of murder?"

Traylor didn't waste time thinking. He nodded and downed his glass, filling it again from the pitcher right away. "Probably. It was like a gradual decline, you know? He was quiet and brooding when I first had him and then when he came back, there was something darker about him. And then the third time, he'd gone way the hell off the rails. I actually watched him fall apart in stages, you know? That's why I guess I wasn't too surprised to hear from the FBI," he said. "In the back of my head, I've been expecting something to come up concerning *Chester* for quite some time now. That he was either dead or had gotten involved in some shit. I guess he finally snapped completely, huh? Did he actually kill someone?"

"We can't say yet," Kate said, getting to her feet.

"Just as well," Traylor said. "The less I know about him, the better."

As if on cue, he turned his attention back to the televisions behind the bar. He did not look sad, but certainly not upset, either. Kate thought he looked emotionless—as if he had long ago given up on his nephew.

And maybe that's why he ended up the way he did, Kate thought. *Foster families gave up on him, as did his own father and uncle. All of that can build and build until something just flat out snaps...*

Thinking that, she thought maybe Al Traylor didn't quite look emotionless. Instead, he looked like a man who considered it a defeat that he had not been strong enough to save someone he once cared about—especially now that the someone in question could very well be convicted of multiple murders.

CHAPTER TWENTY THREE

Because Whip Springs was less than half an hour from the bar that Al Traylor had chosen, Kate decided to pay Chester Black a visit despite the time. It was 9:47 when they came to the dirt road that led back to a small cluster of mobile homes. DeMarco had put a call in to Palmetto to get the address, only to hear Palmetto laughing. He wasn't able to give an actual address, but plenty of detail in his directions.

"He says if you fall off the face of the Earth, we've gone too far," DeMarco commented as Kate turned the car onto the dirt road.

Several feet down the road, they came to a small iron square sitting up on a post. The box contained six smaller boxes inside of it, each listed with a last name. It was a crude little PO box of sorts, apparently so the mail carrier didn't have to go all the way down the extremely poorly paved road. Using the flashlight on her phone, Kate saw that Box #4 was adorned with **C. Black**.

It took about another minute or so before the mobile homes came into view. They were derelict structures, one of which was missing a window and was covered instead with a tattered blue tarp. In one yard, two men sat around a small charcoal grill, drinking beer and eating burgers.

Kate parked the car in front of the fourth trailer. She pulled in behind a very old Chevy Cavalier. The back window was adorned with band logos and a pentagram. Given the stories Al Traylor had just told them, as well as the darkened night and isolated locale, Kate was slightly on edge when she and DeMarco got out of the car. She saw that DeMarco was also looking around cautiously, her hand resting by her side where her Glock was concealed beneath her jacket.

The steps leading up to Chester Black's rickety wooden porch were nothing more than concrete blocks that had been strategically stacked to make a crude set of stairs. As they neared them, DeMarco took two quick strides, taking the lead. Several years ago, this might have offended Kate. But now it seemed almost polite—a way to get in front of any potential danger to assist a partner who was twenty-seven years her senior.

When they took the steps, Kate caught a pungent odor. Something rotting...maybe a dead cat or a deer that had died out in the woods. She wrinkled her nose at it and continued up the wobbly stairs.

The two agents gave one another a nod of readiness before DeMarco knocked on the aluminum screen door.

"Yeah!" a male voice yelled from inside. "Who is it?"

Not wanting to yell, particularly not to be overheard by the men in the yard two trailers back, Kate leaned in as close to the screen door as she could. "Mr. Black, it's the FBI. We need to speak with you, please."

"Bullshit," came the reply, layered with a laugh.

This was followed by footsteps storming toward the door. The door was opened and a pale, thin man looked out at them. His hair was jet black, as was his shirt. His nose was pierced, as was his bottom lip. A tattoo peeked out of the collar of his shirt, running up his neck to the underside of his chin. A tentacle, from the looks of it.

It was clear that Chester Black had thought someone was playing a joke on him. While he stared at them in confusion, DeMarco took the opportunity to show him her badge. "Like my partner said," DeMarco remarked, "we're with the FBI. We'd like to ask you some questions about recent activity in the area."

"What kind of activity?" he asked, vigilant.

He tried staring them down but his eyes were glassy and distant. Kate was pretty sure he was on something. He had the look of someone coming down off of a pretty strong high.

"We'd really prefer to come inside," Kate said.

"That's not going to happen."

"Fine. Then we can talk out here and I can raise my voice a bit so those gentlemen in the yard two trailers up can hear what we need to ask you."

"You think I care what those rednecks think of me?"

"I don't know," DeMarco said. "But I know what *you're* going to think of me if you make me go all the way back to the PD and get a warrant to come into this pigsty. Make it easy on everyone, *Chester*. And we know that's not your real name. We know your real name. We can broadcast that during our conversation on the porch, too."

Black looked at odds, torn in his decision. "Shit," he said. "Fine. Come in. But I clearly wasn't expecting company. Especially not the fucking FBI."

"You high on something right now?" Kate asked.

He only sneered at her as they passed through the doorway.

When they walked inside, the first thing Kate noticed was the smell. It was the same thing she had smelled outside, only stronger. She could not decide if Chester Black simply needed to empty his trash or if some woodland creature had found its way under the trailer and died.

"So what do you want?" Black asked. He was still standing by the door, basically trapping them inside. *Or making sure he has a clear path to escape,* Kate thought, bringing Davey Armstrong to mind.

"You live about fifteen miles away from the Langley family," Kate said. "They fostered you when you were a kid, right?"

"Yeah. For like three months, before they shipped me off to another family."

"Did you know they had been killed?"

Black nodded. "I heard it from one of my neighbors. Murdered, right?" After a short pause, he rolled his eyes and laughed. "Ah, shit. You think I did it?"

"There's no accusation here," DeMarco said. "We're just trying to get as much information as we can. For instance, did you know the Nashes had been murdered, too?"

The look on his face was one of pure shock. But something about it did not sit well with Kate. It didn't seem like he was shocked at the news. It was almost as if someone had discovered some secret and he had not expected it to be revealed.

"No, I hadn't."

"On top of that," Kate said, "a woman named Monica Knight was murdered within the last thirty-six hours."

"You stayed with her for a bit, too, correct?" DeMarco said.

Now there was bewilderment in his eyes. "What the hell? And you're here…why, exactly?"

"You stayed with all three of them at some point in time. And based on some of the things we've gathered from your family members…"

"My uncle, you mean?"

Kate ignored this and went on. "Mr. Black, could you provide your whereabouts for each night over the last week or so?"

"I've been all over the place. Roanoke one night. I was at a friend's place last night in Vinton."

"Can you provide proof?"

"Other than word of mouth?"

"That will do for now," DeMarco said. "But we'd eventually need more."

"If you are claiming that you are not the person behind the murders," Kate said, "would you care to tell me what you know about the victims? Is there anything else that might possibly connect them?"

"Other than the fact that I was too much for them to handle?" Black said. "And that Bethany Langley knew how to throw a right-handed slap like a fucking MMA fighter? Yeah, I'm sorry they're dead and all. But fuck them. They gave up on me a long time ago. And the Nashes in particular were so holier-than-thou, it was sickening. Looks to me like it was karma; looks like they got what they deserved."

"That seems a little harsh," DeMarco said.

"Harsh? Harsh! How about that bitch Monica...dumping me back with DSS after she found out that I had been sexually abused by one of my foster dads. Too much for her too handle. And the Nashes...when I told them I might be interested in boys...another family just dumping me off. Getting slapped every time I dared to question the Langleys. Loving homes my ass..."

While Black went on his little tirade, Kate started to slowly study the trailer. There was a small steak knife sitting on the scarred end table by the couch. At the sight of the knife, the smell of the place grew all the more alarming.

"You may want to put a lid on that kind of talk if you want us to believe that you had nothing to do with the murders," DeMarco said. "You could be one hundred percent innocent, and that sort of talk will get you a nice spot in an interrogation room."

"You going to arrest me for talking bad about someone?" Black yelled.

But Kate barely registered this. Instead, she was looking at part of something white under the couch. She walked over to it and saw that it was the corner of a towel. She reached down and grabbed it.

"What are you doing?" Black asked.

Kate pulled it out and took a quick step back. The towel was crumpled, filthy, and matted with blood.

Fresh blood.

"What's this?" Kate asked.

"I hurt myself earlier," Black said. "Nasty cut. That towel was the first thing I grabbed."

"And why is it shoved under the couch?" DeMarco asked.

"Let me see the cut," Kate said. She felt her right hand inching toward her sidearm.

"It's in an area I'd rather not show some random ass FBI agent," Black said. "And I know my rights. You can't demand that I remove my clothing to show you a wound."

"Then explain yourself," DeMarco said. She was doing a little less to hide the fact that she was thinking of going for her gun.

"Get out of my house," he spat. "Go get that warrant."

"Explain the blood," Kate said. She kept looking back at it. It was a lot of blood, but not too much to automatically make her assume the worst.

"I'm not explaining anything. I said get the fuck out of my house!"

Kate fought her instincts and acted. She was going to lie but she figured that was okay. Black had claimed to know his rights. But for someone dumb enough to quickly shove a blood-soaked towel under his couch, she had to wonder. She figured she could test it just enough to stay out of any legal trouble.

"Apparently, you *don't* know your rights," she said. "That much fresh blood being present at a location where we are questioning someone in an active murder investigation trumps your rights. In fact," she said, showing him her gun but not yet drawing it, "it could be considered threatening materials. Enough for us to draw our weapons and bring you in. Now...*explain yourself!*"

The way his eyes darted in worry made it very apparent that he had bought her dishonesty. He shook his head nervously and then shrugged. "Fine..."

And then he threw an elbow hard into DeMarco's chest.

She coughed and stumbled back into the kitchen. She slipped on the linoleum and banged into the fridge. Black then made a mistake in gauging Kate's actions; he took a split second to see how she was going to follow up before he moved. Had he instantly gone for the door and into the night, he might have escaped. But he hesitated, toying with the idea of attacking Kate as well.

Before he could take a single step forward, Kate was rushing at him. It was all too familiar to the scene at Davey Armstrong's apartment. Black's mistake, though, was that in seeing her coming forward, he decided to defend himself.

He reached for the knife on the end table in one deft move. But as his hand fell on it, Kate brought her elbow down on his forearm. Black screamed and went to the floor like a sack of rocks. DeMarco was there with her in an instant, throwing her arms around Black's torso as he tried to fight them off.

But he was far too frail and weak. Kate had him cuffed within five seconds. And as she got to her feet, her heart thrumming, she looked back at the towel.

That blood was very fresh and she'd be willing to bet just about anything that it had not come from Chester Black.

CHAPTER TWENTY FOUR

Kate and DeMarco had searched the area around the trailer for any signs of where the blood had come from but found nothing. DeMarco had found where the stench from within the house had come from, though. There had indeed been a dead cat beneath the trailer. In fact, there had also been a dead dog as well. The dog had been very recently killed, a slit tearing it open from its jaw to its hips.

Kate was thankful that the media had not discovered this grisly tidbit. Somehow, they had learned about Black's arrest; when they arrived at the police department in Roanoke, there were already two news vans parked outside, waiting, with a third roaring down the street in search of a place to park.

As Kate and DeMarco quickly escorted Black into the station, Palmetto came rushing up to them with an apologetic look on his face.

"How the hell did the media find out about this?" Kate barked at him.

"No clue. The chief is pissed. He's got an active hunt for the leak. Sadly, it's happened far too often around here before."

This did nothing to decrease Kate's irritation. She hustled Black into the station through the back door where there were already two reporters jockeying for position. She didn't bother so much as looking at them as they passed by, though she did hear their questions.

"Is this the killer?"

"Why did he do it?"

"Are there more victims out there?"

Inside, things were just as chaotic. There were officers fielding phone calls, basically screaming at the people on the other end as they asked for information regarding the suspect.

Palmetto jockeyed in behind them as they escorted Black down the hall. As they made their way down, the Chief of Police met them coming from the other direction. He looked flustered and tired, but altogether relieved.

"This is him?" the chief asked. "This is the killer?"

"I didn't kill anyone!" Black screamed.

"Just lead us to an interrogation room," Kate said.

Somewhere within her heart, she felt a pang of sorrow—a tearing sensation. She could not make sense of it, but whatever it was made her think of Michelle and Melissa.

"You okay?" DeMarco asked.

Kate nodded. "Hey, follow them to interrogation, would you? I need to take a moment."

"Sure," DeMarco said, looking concerned.

Kate raced back down the hall, to where they had passed a restroom several moments ago. She went in, grateful to find it empty. She gathered her breath and stared at herself in the mirror, wondering just what in the hell was happening to her. Panic attack? Adrenaline surge? No…none of that seemed right.

You know what this is, she told herself. *There's a part of you—the grandmother part, probably—that doesn't think you should be here. That part of you thinks you should be back in Richmond, within a call and twenty miles or so of your daughter and granddaughter. This is guilt…guilt of not being readily accessible to your family even in your supposed retirement.*

A tear trailed down her cheek unexpectedly. She wiped it away as she pulled out her phone. She toyed with calling Melissa but figured it was too late. Instead, she sent a text. She typed it in quickly, taken aback by this sudden surge of emotion.

Ironically, being back on the job is making me miss you guys even more. I hope you can understand this back and forth with my work. More importantly, I hope you can forgive me. Give that baby girl a kiss from her grandma. Love you.

She pocketed the phone and checked herself over in the mirror. She certainly couldn't question Chester Black looking like an emotional mess. Confident that she had herself under control, she walked back toward the hallway.

Just as she reached the door, her phone dinged from her pocket. She dug it out and saw that Melissa had already answered her. She imagined her daughter at home, sitting in bed with her husband and maybe scrolling through Facebook on her phone. Michelle would be sleeping in her crib in the bedroom down the hall. The thought brought a smile to her face.

Melissa's response read: **I don't understand it, but that's ok. You're passionate about your job, and that's a good thing. Get out there and get it done, Mom. I have to raise my daughter in this world…so make it a safer one. Go get the bad guys.**

Kate let out a little chuckle.

Go get the bad guys.

She pushed the restroom door open and walked quickly down the hall to do exactly that.

***

Kate could tell that the hard façade that Chester Black was putting up was a fake one. There was a terror in his eyes that was much like that of a child staring down the dark cellar stairs during a thunderstorm.

As Kate entered the interrogation room, DeMarco was standing on one side of the table with Black sitting on the other side. "...and forensics is going to tell us pretty quickly where that blood on the towel came from," DeMarco was saying. "So you may as well tell us now."

"You found the animals under the trailer, didn't you?" Black said with a scowl.

"So it was from the dog?" DeMarco said.

"Yes."

Kate thought about the knife she'd seen on the end table. She wondered how much time had passed between his brutal act and DeMarco knocking on his door. Something about the idea chilled her.

"Your uncle told us that he thought you were into some satanic things," Kate said. "Would animal sacrifice be one of them?"

Black glared up at her, that scowl trembling. "No one understands it, but it's not a crime, is it?"

"It can be. You can throw the religious rights stuff at us to keep us tied up for a while but if we really want to pin it on you, we could. Just being honest."

"I did it around eight o'clock," Black said. "The sacrifice. And the bodies...I keep them for about two days."

"So the cat body we found..."

"Last night," Black said.

"Forgive the ignorance, but is there no church?" DeMarco asked. "Do you just do these things solo at home?"

"I meet with others at a location once every month. It's not a *church*, but a gathering."

"And you sacrifice animals there?" Kate asked.

"Yes."

"Dogs and cats?"

"Sheeps and goats."

"Ever do any human sacrifices?" DeMarco asked. She was really digging into him, apparently feeling that even if this satanic stuff was true, Black was very much still the killer.

Kate then realized that about five seconds had passed since DeMarco had asked him about human sacrifices. "Answer the question, Mr. Black," Kate said.

"I've never killed a person before," Chester said. "I'm well aware that satanists have that stereotype, but it's mostly just bullshit."

It didn't quite sit right with Kate. If he was practicing some religious sacrifice, why come at them so aggressively? Did he know he'd be looking at animal cruelty charges at the very least?

Kate was about to continue with her questioning when someone came knocking at the door. DeMarco answered it and a hurried-looking man entered. He held a sheet of paper in his hand. His other was clenched into a fist.

"A moment outside, Agents?" the man said.

Kate and DeMarco walked out of the room with him. The moment the door was closed behind them, the man started in.

"He's our guy," he said. He then seemed to forget who he was and what he was doing. He shook his head and said: "Sorry. I'm Neil Banner, pathology. There are two blood types on the towel we took from his house. One is canine in nature. But the other is human. We don't have a positive ID on the blood and may never get one. It's too contaminated."

"But you're certain it's human?" Kate asked.

"One hundred percent certain," he said, handing her the report.

She nodded and took the paper. "Thank you."

With that, she walked back into the interrogation room. She felt like she was being propelled on a rocket. Though it seemed anticlimactic, they'd gotten him. Their killer was sitting right in front of them.

"You have one chance to change your story, Mr. Black. You're certain there's just dog blood on that towel?"

"Yes!" He nearly screamed it.

Kate placed the report on the table. She was sure he wouldn't be able to understand any of it, but she wanted him to know that they now had proof.

"That was your last chance. The bad news for you is that an officer will come in here very shortly and read you your rights. You will be under arrest for probable murder. The good news is that I won't be the one doing it. Because the things I've seen these last few days…if it was you that did them, I kind of want to hurt you right now."

There was plenty more she wanted to say, mainly because there was still some seed of doubt in the back of her mind. It seemed too easy, almost like it was handed to them. But the report on the table showed human blood on that towel…a towel Chester Black had tried to hide from them.

You're overthinking things again, she told herself. *You got him. Consider it a job well done and get home. Go see Melissa and Michelle.*

"Anything else to add, Agent DeMarco?" Kate asked.

"No. I'm good."

"Enjoy your time in prison," Kate told Black. "I'm sure you'll get life, but I doubt the judicial system will let you live it. Five victims…gruesome murders. You do the math."

"I don't know what the fuck you're talking about!" Black screamed.

And damn if Kate didn't see genuine confusion and horror in his eyes.

Don't go there, she said. *This is your guy. He's partially insane and the report right there on the table spells out his guilt.*

That thought was enough to allow her to leave the room. DeMarco followed her out and cut her off in the hallway.

"Agent Wise…Kate…are you okay?"

"Yeah, why?"

"I've never seen you so pissed at someone before. That got raw. Just checking in on you."

"Yeah, I'm fine. Honestly…I just want to go home."

"Let's do that," DeMarco said. "We got our man. Maybe we can sneak out before paperwork starts. I think the local PD can handle that on their own."

"Sounds good to me," Kate said.

They walked down the hallway toward the front of the police department. When Kate realized she could faintly hear the screams of Chester Black proclaiming his so-called innocence, she was surprised at just how easily she was able to tune it out.

CHAPTER TWENTY FIVE

Neither of them even considered staying in a motel in Roanoke. Kate and DeMarco figured they could take shifts driving if the other got tired. They did indeed switch out, DeMarco taking the wheel a little less than halfway through the trip so Kate could doze. Kate was stirred awake by DeMarco tapping on her shoulder.

Kate opened her eyes, instantly noticing the pain in her neck from sleeping in the passenger's seat.

"You're home," DeMarco said.

Sure enough, Kate looked out of the window and saw her house. She checked her watch and saw that it was 4:05 in the morning.

"Thanks," Kate said. "Now, come on in. I'm not letting you drive back to DC or try checking into a motel at such an hour."

"You sure?"

"Positive," Kate said. She got out of the car and started toward her steps before DeMarco could argue.

Kate didn't see the point in being formal. With what she and DeMarco had been through—not just with this case but with the one they'd shared two months ago—they were, as far as Kate was concerned, quite close.

"Guest bedroom is down the hall, last door on the right," she said. "The bathroom is right beside that. Make yourself at home. And if you wake me up early for anything, you might just get shot."

DeMarco smiled and headed down the hall. She turned back to Kate and smiled. "Seriously," she said, "thanks. It's been an absolute pleasure and thrill to get to know you, Agent Wise."

"I'll return the sentiment in the morning," Kate said. "For now...sleep."

With that, Kate walked down the same hallway and entered her bedroom. She stripped down, quickly ruled out a shower, and fell into bed. She had just enough time to wonder if DeMarco would be comfortable in her house before sleep reached up and snatched her.

***

While DeMarco did not wake up Kate up the next morning, the smell of brewing coffee did. Kate tried to ignore it, but she had always been as sucker for a good cup of morning coffee. She looked at the alarm clock on her bedside table and saw that it was 9:45. She figured six hours of sleep was enough for now; she could easily make up for it tonight.

She rolled out of bed, threw on her around-the-house clothes, and headed out to the kitchen. DeMarco was already showered and dressed. She sat at the kitchen bar, scrolling through her phone with a cup of coffee sitting beside her. When she saw Kate enter the kitchen, she looked up and gave a nearly apologetic look.

"Sorry," she said. "You told me to make myself at home. I figured that meant coffee was included."

"Yes. And thank you for brewing it. How long have you been up?"

"About an hour. I called Duran and filled him in on everything."

"We did that last night…"

"Oh, I know. I mean I told him I crashed here because of the late hour. He seemed cool with it."

"Oh. Okay."

"If you don't mind, I'm going to finish up my coffee and get out of your hair."

"You're not in my hair. It's nice to have the company."

"Oh, I don't really have a choice. Duran wants me there this afternoon to give a briefing."

"You need me to come?" Kate asked.

"That's not necessary. Consider it one of the perks of your current position."

Kate knew that DeMarco meant it as a funny little jab with no ill intent but it stung nonetheless. She went to the coffeemaker and poured herself a cup. She was quite happy to find that it did not feel odd to be sharing her home with DeMarco. In fact, it felt natural.

"When you get back, will you keep me posted on how it goes down? I'd really like to see this one to the end."

"Of course." DeMarco sipped from her coffee with a thoughtful look on her face. "You don't feel comfortable leaving now, do you? You don't think it's Black."

"I don't know. It fits…especially the human blood on that towel. The whole satanic thing just feels too…convenient. I'd love to see what the lab results come back reading."

"Yeah. I thought so, too."

They left it at that, the question hanging in the air above them. As Kate joined DeMarco at the bar with her coffee, she thought of Black trying to escape his trailer. She thought of the terrible smell, of the blood and the animal carcasses under the trailer.

It's him, she thought. *Sometimes life hands you an answer and you just have to take it.*

Yes, some other more stubborn part of her thought. *But sometimes life forces those answers on you whether you want them or not.*

***

DeMarco was gone by 10:30, leaving Kate alone with her thoughts for the first time since DeMarco had knocked on her door to start the case off a few nights ago. Unsurprisingly, those thoughts led to Michelle and Melissa. She sat on her front porch, enjoying the quiet hum of the Carytown district and the morning's third cup of coffee, and doing her best to figure out how to manage her life from here on out.

It started by having a chat with Melissa. It wasn't something she dreaded, but it also wasn't something she was particularly looking forward to, either. She figured she may as well get it over with. Besides…she tended to blow things out of proportion when it came to Melissa. For all she knew, her daughter might not be too upset with how things had gone down at all. She'd basically said as much during their brief text exchange the night before.

Go get the bad guys, Melissa had texted.

Again, Kate thought of Chester Black and started to feel any certainty she'd had wavering.

Before it could consume her mind, she picked up her cell phone and placed a call to Melissa. Melissa answered on the second ring. When Kate said "Hello," she could hear Michelle babbling in the background.

"Hey, Lissa. Thought I'd let you know I'm back home."

"Oh, good. Did you get the bad guy?"

"We think so. Thanks for that text, by the way. I know that conversation could have gone very differently. I appreciated the kindness."

"Don't mention it. Mom…please don't take this the wrong way, but I'm used to it. You were always like this when I was a kid, you know? I didn't automatically think some switch was going to flip when you became a grandmother."

"Well, maybe you should have."

128

"Don't be too hard on yourself, Mom. Yes, I was pissed when you called at the last minute to tell me that we had to cut short our first night out in two months because you'd been called into work. But it rolled off my back—eventually."

"Thank you, Lissa."

"Of course. But listen. You have to understand that I need to start planning accordingly. Until you can *really* retire, I don't think I'm going to ask you to babysit anymore." She stopped here, perhaps waiting for some protest. Kate felt one coming, but wanted to give Melissa a chance to explain first. "We're going to look for one of those certified babysitters, you know? Our five-year anniversary is coming up in three months and we're thinking of taking two days to ourselves. And I love you, Mom...but until the job comes second, I don't feel like I can ask you to keep Michelle."

"That hurts, but it's fair."

"Don't get me wrong. Michelle and I would love to come over and visit—a lot. I want her to know you. I really do. I keep telling her you had to bail because even in retirement, you're being a badass."

"That's a rosy way to paint it, I suppose."

"Don't sweat it, Mom. Look, how about Michelle and I come over on Saturday. We'll do lunch and I'll let you change some of these disgusting diapers."

"Sounds like a plan," Kate said. With the conversation coming to a close, the weight of it was indeed starting to sting.

She doesn't see me as reliable enough to keep my own granddaughter, she thought. *And the hell of it is that she has a good point.*

She stared out to the street, watching the pedestrian traffic and thinking about their individual lives. They'd all go home at some point today and either lift up or tear down their friends and family members. They would go home to feel loved or feel as if they weren't quite good enough.

That's every life, she thought. *The idea of being happy is probably different for each one of them. For some it rests in work; in others, friends, family, or lovers. In others, some unnamable thing.*

It was a thought that made her realize that if she was ever going to balance her life in a way that allowed her to keep her feet in the pools of the FBI while still being a reliable mother and grandmother, she was going to have to finally scrutinize that part of her own life. What was it that made her truly happy? And if it was more than one thing, what did she need to do to bring those two worlds together?

With this heavy thought on her mind, her cell phone buzzed at her. She checked it and saw that it was a text from Allen.

Are you back in town? Want to do dinner again? All the stuff that happened after dinner last time not expected. ☺

Kate couldn't suppress the giggle that came out of her in response to the little smiley face and the innuendo of how their last date had ended. She thought for a moment, smiled, and then sent a response.

I am home. But tired...got in late and need to catch up on sleep. How about dinner tomorrow? The only stipulation being that all the stuff that happened after dinner last night is also included.

It felt good to be back in the dating saddle, she had to admit. It had been a very long time since she had spoken to a man in such a way. It made her feel about twenty years younger.

Allen responded right away. **Jeez, twist my arm why don't you? Sounds good. See you at 6?**

She quickly returned a text to confirm the time and then headed back inside. She looked around the empty house and felt a little surge of warmth. She had a date lined up for tomorrow, lunch with Michelle and Melissa next week, and she had just come back from presumably wrapping a gruesome murder case. Life was looking pretty sweet.

Then why does something feel off?

It was a good question. And the reason it unsettled her so much was because in asking herself the question, Chester Black kept coming to mind.

What if it's not him?

And it was that question that had her sitting in her armchair, staring at the walls. She sat there for a very long time and with each second that passed, she started to wonder if she and DeMarco had left Roanoke too soon.

CHAPTER TWENTY SIX

Even though she'd told Allen their date would have to wait until tomorrow because she was so tired, Kate ended up making full use of her afternoon. As three o'clock rolled around, she walked several blocks down the street for Chinese takeout. Then, over orange chicken and cheese wontons, she pulled the case files up on her computer and took out the few printed materials she had collected while in Roanoke. She made herself a little workstation at the kitchen table and went to work, trying to alleviate the nasty feeling that Chester Black was not their man and the case was still wide open.

The thing that was really hanging her up was the blanket. And that made no sense to her. It was clear that it had meaning to the killer. It took a lot of extra effort to cram it into the throats of his victims and it was clear that he was doing it on purpose.

But the question remained: *Why?*

She thought of Chester Black again. She thought of the personality he projected and the things they had seen and experienced in his trailer. Kate was far from a psychologist but she didn't seen any outright signs from him of someone who might still be clutching to some long-lost memories of his childhood that involved a blanket.

She recalled what Danielle Ethridge had said, about how the blanket had once likely been a comfort object. And as far as Kate was concerned, Chester Black did not seem like the type to obsess over a comfort object.

The crimes Chester Black had committed, while absolutely deplorable and poorly thought out, were of what he felt was necessity—crimes that were tied into his abnormal religious beliefs. That in no way made him a killer.

But they found human blood on that towel. What about that?

That was the one roadblock in keeping Kate from thinking Chester Black was innocent. If she could get around that, she would have to face the fact that she was pretty sure she and DeMarco had left for home, leaving the wrong man in a holding cell in Roanoke.

If the blanket was a comfort object...what does that say about the killer when he was a kid?

She dwelled on this for a moment, sensing there was something worth digging into. If the killer held onto a security blanket as a child, it likely meant that he'd been insecure. Maybe even quiet. Again, she was not a psychologist, but she had been involved with enough cases to make extremely educated guesses—which usually turned out to be right.

Yet they had spent their time looking for someone who was violent by nature. They had been looking for a child who had dealt with issues from a young age. But what if their killer had never truly seemed violent until just recently? What if their killer had been a quiet and mostly harmless kid, dragging a blanket around behind him?

She'd been digging through the files for any evidence of this for a little over an hour when her cell phone rang. She saw that it was DeMarco and answered it right away.

"All wrapped up?" Kate asked.

"On this end, yes. But I got a call during the meeting. It was Palmetto, from Roanoke."

"The human blood on the towel…"

"That really has been bothering you, huh?" DeMarco said.

"It has. Anyway…what were the results?"

"The blood was from a woman named Abby Warren. Roanoke PD ran a search and found her alive and well. She happens to be Chester Black's girlfriend. And she admitted to the two of them engaging in some consensual blood-letting during sex."

"Cutting one another?"

"Yeah. She has the scars to prove it. Chester figured he'd be charged for something because he was the one doing the cutting, so he never said anything. But it all checks out. And based on all of this…"

"He's free to go."

"Well, he's looking at some animal cruelty charges, but it's not looking like he's our killer."

"So what now?"

"What now is you rest up. I'll pick you up around nine in the morning tomorrow and we're heading back to Roanoke."

"We have to start with Dr. Ethridge," Kate said. "I think we've been looking for the wrong kind of killer." She then told DeMarco about her breakthrough concerning a quiet kid that, for some reason or another, had become violent more recently rather than always having an appetite for it.

"Sounds like a plan," DeMarco said. "Just…well, this isn't going to mess up any babysitting plans again, is it?"

"No. Just a date." She frowned when she thought about having to cancel on Allen again. At least this time she'd have the awareness to inform him beforehand.

"You okay heading back out there?" DeMarco asked.

Kate appreciated the respect and courtesy but once again felt that she was being handed certain privileges. She knew that if she elected not to return to Roanoke to put a bow on this case, Duran would likely not come down too hard on her. But she *wanted* to go out there, to help DeMarco find the killer before he could strike again.

"Absolutely," she said. "I'll have coffee waiting when you pick me up."

They ended the call and rather than call it a day, Kate went directly back to her case files. Maybe there was something they had missed. Maybe if she now looked at it through the lens of looking for a killer who had been quiet and introverted as a child, something new would present itself.

She wanted to be in the know, the details of the case like the lyrics to a well-worn song in her head. Because if she had her way, they were going to catch the bastard this time.

Maybe even quickly enough so that she could keep her date with Allen.

CHAPTER TWENTY SEVEN

True to her word, Kate had coffee waiting the next morning. She knew that DeMarco took it black, so she went ahead and poured some into an insulated cup. DeMarco arrived twenty minutes late but Kate was fine with that. She realized the ungodly hour DeMarco had to leave DC in order to arrive at her house so early, so she was willing to overlook the tardiness. Not that she had any authority to give her grief over it anyway.

DeMarco seemed troubled almost right away. Kate volunteered to drive, allowing DeMarco to wrestle with her thoughts. But after a while, it was just too much to bear. They were comfortable enough with one another now where silence among them was perfectly okay, but this one was thick and filled with anxiousness.

"What's on your mind?" Kate asked.

"Chester Black. I was so sure it was him."

"It was a safe assumption," Kate said. "And you know what? I felt unsure about him from the start. I should have said something."

"Yeah, but even if you had, we'd be right back here…right where we are now. Chasing our tails and not sure where to look. All you would have saved was a night in an interrogation room for Chester Black. And let's face it—he sort of deserved it."

"Is this the first time you've been wrong about something on a case?" Kate asked.

"God no."

"And it won't be the last, either. Don't let it bother you so much."

DeMarco nodded, but still gazed out the window with a brooding look on her face. Kate understood it. She, too, was beating herself up by not fully investing in the bit of hesitation she had felt when they left Roanoke. But she had also experienced this enough in her career to know that it was useless to ponder on it and keep looking back. If they obsessed over things that happened in the past, that gave the killer an edge in the present.

And this killer already seemed to have more than enough of an edge.

***

Dr. Ethridge appeared a little rushed when Kate and DeMarco showed up at her office at 1:40. She had been expecting them, as DeMarco had called on their way down to Roanoke to keep her abreast of what was happening. But there was a sense of urgency to the doctor now, as if she too could feel the absolute intensity and importance of the situation.

"I've blocked off the next two hours in my schedule to help any way I can," Ethridge said. "I've looked through all of my records over the past fifteen years and pulled any file that seemed like it would be a match. Unfortunately, there's quite a bit."

She pointed to a pile of folders on her desk. It sat about a foot and a half tall. It was certainly quite a bit of material to sift through, but not as bad as Kate had been expecting. "That doesn't look too bad," she commented.

"Oh, this is only the physical records," she said. "This is everything from 2003 back. Everything from 2004 to current day is saved digitally on the server. There's this physical pile and then about thirty more on the server."

"Will you allow us access to the server?" DeMarco asked.

"Normally, I'd put up a fight. But this situation is getting out of hand."

"Thank you," Kate said. "Agent DeMarco, would you like to take the digital files while I go through the folders?"

"That works."

"Dr. Ethridge, I'd like to have you on hand to answer any questions that might arise."

"Of course. Now, these files that I have pulled—as well as the digital ones I have already flagged for you—are based on the profile you gave me. A kid who was very quiet and introverted. The type that might seek comfort from something like a blanket or a stuffed animal."

"That's correct," Kate said.

"It's worth noting that most children that fit that profile are going to be the type who would respond more to a mother-figure rather than a father-figure. Because of that, I pulled files with patients with that characteristic as well."

"Incredible work," DeMarco said. "Now, is there a computer I can work from?"

"Yes, you can use my personal laptop," Ethridge said. She went to her desk, opened it up, and logged DeMarco in.

The next half an hour felt very much like an intense study session to Kate. It reminded her of her earlier days with the bureau when she had often been stuck with painstaking research assignments. Even back then, though, she'd been seen as an excellent profiler. It was one of the reasons it was bothering her so badly that she could not easily pin down the killer in this case. Even as she went through Ethridge's files and started ruling patients out based on the date of service, she knew full well that the answer may not be here.

She fished through the folders as DeMarco clicked through the files on Ethridge's laptop. Most of the files contained at least one Polaroid picture of the patient. Many of them looked into the camera without much of an expression, though some had bright smiles on their faces. She nearly asked Ethridge why she kept these pictures but remembered somewhere along the way in her profiler training that psychologists often used this technique to show their patients how an expression could speak volumes. It was a great conversation starter. *Why do you feel this way today? The little boy in this picture doesn't look very happy, does he?*

Kate also noticed that in a few of the thicker folders, Ethridge had kept drawings that the children had made. Some were quite pretty in a childlike way—perfectly square houses with triangular roofs with big fluffy clouds and bright suns in the skies. But there were some that were clear cries for help: stick-figure kids with frowning faces, crimson pools around little feet, hard red and black lines everywhere.

"Do you have every child draw something for you?" Kate asked.

"Most of the time," Ethridge answered. "It really all depends on the level of trauma they are dealing with. Simple little drawings are a great way for me to really get a quick judge of their emotional state. It gives me topics to start from without having to guess."

"How often do you get ones like this?" Kate asked. She held up a picture of a little girl in pigtails. Behind her, a little dog had been drawn upside down. Something was on fire behind all of it. The little girl's mouth was a big black O and tears were coming out of her eyes in big exaggerated drops.

"About half the time."

"Is there any correlation between these types of drawings and the kind of kid we're looking for in all these files?"

"Sometimes. The kids that are quiet and reserved tend to draw somber pictures, but nothing violent. Of course, that's not *always* the case. While the diagnoses can be the same, there are no two kids that are one hundred percent alike in how they handle their emotions. So one introverted child might draw rain clouds or big storm clouds with lightning while another might draw a man with a knife or a dead animal. There's no right-down-the-middle with this sort of thing."

Kate nodded, putting the drawing back with a little chill creeping down her spine. DeMarco then called Ethridge over to the computer with a question. As the two of them chatted, Kate continued to go through the folders. She saw ruined childhood after ruined childhood and she started to get sentimental. Any one of these kids could be Melissa. No kid was guaranteed a safe childhood. No child could be promised a healthy and happy life.

This stark realization came to a grinding halt when Kate opened the next folder in the pile. Like a few others, the child's Polaroid was up front, paper-clipped to the primary summary file. It was a picture of a boy giving a very thin smile that was clearly being forced. Kate guessed him to be about eight years old. Maybe nine at most.

She skimmed the file but when she realized it was quite thick, she looked up at Dr. Ethridge. "What can you tell me about this patient?" she asked.

Ethridge came over and looked at the file. She fingered the Polaroid in a loving sort of way and frowned. "That's Jeremy Neely. I saw him for about three years."

"Was he an orphan?"

"He was bounced around a few foster homes in his youth, yes. Poor kid…he was seven years old when he watched his father kill his mother. He hit her in the head with a bat right in front of Jeremy. He walked around his dead mother's body for almost an entire day before anyone knew what had happened."

"My God," Kate said.

DeMarco had taken interest now as well. She was looking up from her laptop, sensing that something might be taking shape. Kate waved her over to join her, feeling that this was finally the break they had been looking for.

"Dr. Ethridge, can you get me the list of foster families he stayed with?"

"I don't have the complete list. You'd have to contact Social Services to get the entire list."

"You have the appropriate clearance to get it, right?"

"I do," Ethridge said slowly. She grabbed her cell phone from her desk as understanding started to bloom in her eyes. She turned her back to the agents and placed the call.

Kate nodded, expecting as much. She then pointed to the picture of Jeremy Neely, making sure DeMarco was seeing the one peculiar thing she had seen.

"Look familiar?" Kate asked.

"Oh my God," DeMarco said. "This is him, isn't it?"

Kate didn't have to answer.

In the picture, little Jeremy Neely held something in his right hand. He clutched it tightly to his side in a tight fist.

A blanket. A blanket with a pattern that Kate and DeMarco had gotten to know quite well.

Ethridge joined them again. There was an annoyed look of panic in her eyes. "They're going to call me back. That's considered private information and even in a situation like this, it has to be cleared. If he was wrapped up in a special-needs domestic abuse or criminal case of any kind, that might be why his name wasn't on the original list of kids—if, that is, he stayed with Ms. Knight, the Nashes, and the Langleys. I pushed hard, though. What would usually take a day or so to get, we should have in a few hours."

"Are you kidding me?" DeMarco said.

"It's a trade-off," Ethridge said. "On the one hand, it's amazing that the government is so dedicated to protecting such information. But on the other hand, they don't bend their rules for much of anything."

"You said you have a partial list, right?" Kate asked.

"Yes, it should be there in the files…"

Ethridge reached in over Kate's shoulder and flipped through the pages. She stopped six pages in and pointed to a section near the bottom. "Right there. It shows where there was a transfer from the Langleys to a group home. But that's all I have. That must have been his first foster home."

The Langleys, Kate thought.

It was more than enough to directly tie the Nashes and Monica Knight.

"If we haven't heard from DSS by the end of the day, I'll get our director to give them a call," Kate said. "As for now, we have a name and that's more than enough. Let's find out where Jeremy Neely lives and pay him a visit."

CHAPTER TWENTY EIGHT

He sat on a large rock, just along the tree line. He stared at the house intently, but patient. He supposed if someone stood on the back porch and stared out in his direction, there was a slight chance that he'd be seen. But he knew their routines well. The only time they ever went out onto the back porch was for their morning coffee and when they grilled something for dinner.

But he knew they were not grilling tonight. In fact, they weren't even home. They'd left two hours ago. He'd barely heard their voices as they'd made their way to the car, arguing between Mexican or Thai for dinner.

Since then, he'd been waiting. He'd sat on the rock, motionless. He was rooted there by the anticipation of what would be happening later. He knew he had a few hours left to wait but that was fine with him. He'd waited nearly twelve years so far...so what was four or five more hours?

This wasn't the first time he'd sat on this rock, watching the house. He'd been here countless times before, watching and learning the ways of their lives.

The Colemans. Harry and Ruth. He had lived under their roof—the very roof he was currently staring at—for about five months at one time. They had been nice enough but, in the end, had not been able to keep him. He supposed he had been too much for them, too much of a hassle for their pretentious well-to-do lives. They'd had busy lives both in and out of the house. When he had come along, though, all of that had changed for them. Their weekend tennis matches: gone. Their Wednesday nights out with friends: also gone.

His eyes traveled from window to window. The one on the right on the second floor was their bedroom. He knew this because one night, they had neglected to shut the blinds as they had readied for bed. He had seen Ruth Coleman's naked body standing right in front of the window for about ten seconds before she had been alert enough to close the blinds. There had been about fifty yards between them but he'd still been able to make out her shape, her curves, the smallish globes of her breasts.

For a woman pushing fifty, it had been quite nice. It was not the first time he had thought of Ruth in a sexual way. There had been one night, when he had lived with them—he had been about ten years old or so at the time—when he had stirred awake from a bad dream. He'd walked down the hall to their room to ask if he could sleep there but had stopped in the doorway when he saw the movement in the bed. Ruth had been sitting up on her knees with Harry beneath her. She'd been making noises that had sounded as if she was in pain but as they moved faster together, he realized that they were sounds of pleasure.

He had watched from the doorway, the door open about a quarter of the way, until they had finished.

He'd held on to that memory, often revisiting it whenever he'd felt the darkness invading his mind. It had almost been enough to make him change his mind about what he had to do.

His thoughts of Ruth's naked body were broken up by the sound of an approaching car. He looked to the driveway and saw their Chrysler rolling in. They parked and got out, laughing. Harry waited for Ruth at the front of the car and took her hand. They walked into the house, giggling.

In the woods, he smiled. Maybe they'd had a few drinks with dinner, maybe just enough to be giddy and horny. Maybe they'd make love sometime in the coming hour or so. He hoped so. Maybe he'd find some way to sneak to a window and watch. Also, if they had been drinking, they'd be good and tired, depleted and conked out by the time he walked out of the tree line and up to their house.

He'd enter through the back door. He knew where the spare key was. He'd spent two hours looking for it one afternoon when he knew they had left for a weekend trip to see Harry's brother in Charlotte, North Carolina. It was in the backyard, underneath one of the boards that served as the border of Ruth's tiny herb garden.

He wanted to go now. He wanted to sneak in and maybe catch them in the act. He had never had sex and had never seen the appeal of it. But all the same, seeing Ruth's body at the window that night had reminded him of his urges. He thought the act itself had to be gross but then again...

No. He had to wait. He knew that. He'd waited this long. No sense in screwing it all up now. He had to wait until it was dark.

As if to tide himself over, he looked into the little rucksack he had set on the ground next to the rock. It had little spatters of dried blood on it. He wasn't sure who it belonged to. Honestly, the last two weeks had been a bloody blur.

He reached into the sack and stroked the handle of the knife.

140

He took out the scrap of old blanket and nuzzled it to his cheek. There was something reassuring about the feel of it, something that told him that everything was going to be okay.

Fully believing that, he placed the scrap back into the sack and waited.

CHAPTER TWENTY NINE

The address Kate had gotten for Jeremy Neely was just on the outskirts of Roanoke, in a tiny little town called Deerborne. The drive itself only took about twenty minutes but because they had spent several hours in Dr. Ethridge's office, it was closing in on 5:30 when Kate and DeMarco pulled up in front of Jeremy Neely's home.

The house was an older two-story house. It was in a low-income neighborhood, the streets uncared for and the lawns mostly dead and gray. An air conditioner unit stuck out of one of the side windows like a rotten tooth about to fall out. It was running, making an awful racket as it leaked a trail of water down the side of the house.

They walked up the concrete stairs and onto the porch. As Kate neared the door, her right hand hovered over the handle of her Glock. She knocked with her left hand. Beside her, DeMarco had locked her legs, ready to spring if necessary.

After ten seconds, no one had answered the door. Kate knocked again, this time saying, "Mr. Neely? Are you home?"

"No car along the street," DeMarco pointed out.

Kate had noticed this as well. She looked up and down the street, weighing their options. They had more than enough reason to believe that Jeremy Neely was their killer. And this had been confirmed as his address. Under any normal circumstances, she might just wait in the car until Neely arrived home. But they were working against a clock here, with no idea whether or not Neely intended to kill again.

"Agent DeMarco, my knees aren't quite what they used to be. Would you mind…?"

DeMarco looked both surprised and honored to have been asked. She drew her Glock, took a step back, and then delivered a hard kick to the door. It sprung open, taking a small portion of the frame with it.

They entered the house in perfect step with one another. Kate took the lead with DeMarco close behind. They stepped quietly, allowing each other to hear the silence of the place. Within a few seconds, Kate felt certain that they were alone; Neely was not here.

Still, they investigated the house with caution, guns at the ready. The living room was sparsely furnished and meticulously cleaned. It offered no clues of any kind. The kitchen was equally useless, revealing nothing more than the fact that Neely needed to do his dishes.

Being that they felt as if every moment wasted was a potentially deadly one for Neely's next target, they skipped everything else in the house and headed directly for the bedroom. Nine times out of ten, that's where clues about any case or suspect were found.

Like the living room, Neely's bedroom was mostly clean and without much furniture or belongings. A queen-sized bed sat along the center of the far wall and a small desk sat beside the bed. Other than an old dresser, that was all there was. Kate checked the closet and found nothing but a few hanging shirts and an empty Amazon box.

When she turned away from the closet, she saw DeMarco crouched on the floor. She was looking under the bed. Apparently, she had found something because she started to reach under it.

"What have you got?" Kate asked.

"A shoebox."

"Careful…"

DeMarco pulled the box out from under the bed. It was unremarkable, identical to just about every other shoebox that had ever been slid under a bed. Kate had done this for her entire life, keeping toys and love letters in it as a girl, and bills and checks as an adult.

They shared an uneasy look as DeMarco opened up the box.

There was only one thing inside.

"Holy shit," Kate breathed.

It an old blanket—a blanket that had clearly been torn from along the sides.

The pattern and fabric was identical to what had been pulled from the throats of the victims. It was also the exact same as the blanket that had been held by Jeremy Neely in the photograph in Ethridge's files.

"Call Duran," Kate said. "We need him to bully whoever the hell is in charge of standing on that foster care information and we need him to do it *now*."

DeMarco pulled her phone from her pocket and did just that. Kate, meanwhile, checked under the bed for anything else but there was nothing to be found.

But the blanket was enough. They had their man now. The only question, of course, was where the hell was he?

You know where he is, she told herself. *He's out targeting his next victim...some other family that tried to help him at some point in their lives and now are being rewarded by being killed.*

On the phone, DeMarco was getting loud with Director Duran's receptionist. "This is an emergency...one he will slaughter you for if you don't get him right now. I don't care *who* he is meeting with!"

That apparently did the trick, as DeMarco was put on hold. She was fuming, pacing around the room in order to do *something* with the pent-up excitement that was rocketing through her body.

Kate felt it, too. The excitement of knowing you were about to break a case...that the endgame was on the horizon.

And knowing that just one phone call separated them from not only apprehending the killer but also potentially saving two lives made it a maddening experience.

She looked back to that tattered blanket as a feeling of dread started to spread through her. Mingled with the excitement, it almost made her feel lightheaded. But the blanket actually helped to ease her mind, to steady her focus.

We've got him, she thought. *We know his name, we know where he lives...we just need to know what other families cared for him as a kid.*

All they could do was wait.

And hope that while they waited, two more people weren't being killed.

***

Kate and DeMarco remained in Neely's house while waiting for the call from Duran. Every minute that passed was excruciating. They both paced the floors, remaining mostly in the bedroom. Kate racked her brain for any other ways to find out who else might have kept Jeremy Neely but could come up with nothing.

"I just don't understand how so many families kept him and no one saw this coming," DeMarco said. "You'd think a murder spree like this one might have been prevented if someone had maybe just paid more attention to the way he acted as a kid."

"You heard Ethridge," Kate said. "No two kids are ever one hundred percent the same. For all we know, Jeremy Neely never showed any signs of doing anything like this."

It reminded Kate of the old adage: It's the quiet ones you need to watch.

Of course, in this scenario, that was absolutely correct.

When Kate's phone rang, both agents went absolutely still for a moment. It had the same effect as a gunshot from the next room. Kate answered it with a jolt of adrenaline blasting through her body.

"This is Agent Wise."

"Wise, it's Duran. I got the list of families. You ready?"

"Shoot."

"In order of appearance, we've got the Langleys, the Nashes, a single woman named Monica Knight, the Colemans, and the Vaughns. But he was only with the Vaughns for two days. He stayed with the Colemans for about five months."

"You got names for the Colemans?" Kate asked.

"And an address. 174 Angler Drive, Moneta, Virginia."

Shit, she thought. *Not local.*

Kate covered the mouthpiece on her phone and looked at DeMarco. "Plug Moneta into your GPS and see how far away it is."

DeMarco did as she was asked. Kate turned her attention back to Duran and asked: "Is that all? No other families?"

"That's it. You think the Colemans are next?" Duran asked.

"It's an incredibly good chance."

DeMarco showed Kate her phone. She had typed Moneta into her map app search bar. It was apparently a little lakeside town about thirty minutes away.

"Moneta is about half an hour away from us," Kate said. "We're headed there now."

"Perfect. Good luck, Wise."

With a nod of understanding between them, Kate and DeMarco sprinted out of the bedroom, through the house, and back outside. As she got behind the wheel, she heard DeMarco on her phone as she got into the passenger seat.

"Palmetto, it's Agent DeMarco. I need you and a few officers to get over to Moneta as soon as possible. Agent Wise and I are headed there now with a strong suspicion that our killer's next target is there."

Kate pulled out into the road and sped forward while DeMarco filled Palmetto in. Dusk was slowly settling down, the horizon holding most of the day's remaining light. When she came to the end of the street, she took a hard right, the back end of the car fishtailing. She felt like she was racing a clock and as far as she was concerned, her time would run out when night fell.

But with a killer so close to her grasp, she'd be damned if she'd let that happen.

CHAPTER THIRTY

Had she not been in a rush to potentially stop a killer, Kate thought she might have enjoyed the quaint and scenic little town of Moneta. It sat alongside Smith Mountain Lake, a lake cupped almost perfectly within the Blue Ridge Mountains. The fact that the sun had pretty much set behind the mountains added a whole new tone of beauty to the place.

As she passed by the central intersection of the town, Kate spotted the two police cruisers in the gas station parking lot to her right. Palmetto had called ahead to Moneta PD and asked for two units to be available for backup while the State PD hurried along. Kate flashed her lights at them as she passed through the intersection and they fell in behind her.

Angler Drive was located within a small subdivision that was separated from the lake by only a thin strip of woodland that grew in size and spread out the closer it got to the mountains. As they crept closer and closer to the Coleman residence, Kate decided on the best approach in her mind. She figured that if Jeremy Neely was indeed there or on the way, there was no sense in scaring him away with blazing sirens and police cars pulling into the driveway. Given that, she elected to park her car along the side of the road just out of eyesight of the Colemans' paved driveway. Behind her, the police cruisers did the same.

When she got out of the car and met one of the officers from the first car as he got out, she realized just how dark it had gotten. She could still see without the aid of a flashlight, but that wouldn't last much longer.

"Thanks for the assist," Kate said. "Agent DeMarco and I will go to the door. If everything is fine and good, that'll be the end of it. We'll inform them of the situation and then ask you to stay here until State PD arrives. You guys can work out the surveillance among yourselves. But if we get in there and find out that we were too late, we'll call for backup."

"Officer Palmetto said this guy has killed five people," the cop said. "Is that true?"

Kate nodded, but thought: *Let's pray it's only five...and not seven.*

* * *

They made their way down the paved drive in a quick walk. They did not want to appear too rushed, nor did they want to seem too casual. As they closed in on the house, Kate noted that a light was on downstairs, shining through the largest window along the front of the house as well as one on the side. Probably the living room. Another one was on upstairs.

There's one good sign, at least, Kate thought.

They ascended the stairs at that same pace but took a moment to collect themselves before Kate knocked on the door. She raised her hand to do just that but was stopped by a noise from somewhere inside.

It was a scream. A man's scream.

Kate tried the front door and found it locked. This door was locked by an electrical lock with a numerical pin—one of the fancier models she'd seen. It was not going to be as easy as knocking the door down at Jeremy Neely's house. Still, DeMarco gave it a try. Her foot slammed into the door and it trembled quite a bit, but it did not pop open.

So much for the element of surprise, Kate thought.

As she leveled her Glock at the lock, another of those screams sounded out. This one was followed by a second sound, more like a low moan, and this one from the throat of a woman.

Turning her head away from the door, she fired off a single round that tore through the lock and the door itself. DeMarco immediately threw another kick, this one blasting the door open.

They entered the house through a small foyer that opened up into the kitchen. And it was right there, in the space between the kitchen and the opening to the living room, that Jeremy Neely was crouched on the floor. In one hand, he held a knife. In the other, he gripped the neck of the man who was pinned under his knees. The man lay beneath him, struggling to get free, but there were a series of cuts on his arms that had weakened him. Already, a pool of blood had started to form on the floor.

A woman lay on the floor as well. She was on her side, blood everywhere, trying to get up but unable to do so.

It took Kate about two second to see all of this and by the time she had taken it all in, DeMarco had sprung to action. Kate was amazed by how fast the woman was. She took two huge strides forward and was then in a crouched position, like an NFL lineman prepared to bowl over the opposition.

148

DeMarco threw herself at Neely, her aim spot on. Her shoulder checked his chest and they both went to the floor in a heap. However, as they fell, DeMarco's left arm jammed down on Neely's knife. Kate saw it happen and she rushed forward, grimacing and hoping that the blade hadn't nicked any arteries.

Neely took advantage of DeMarco's shock and kicked her away. He then raised the knife to plunge it down through DeMarco's chest, but Kate reached him just in time. She drew her knee up hard, connecting with the underside of Neely's jaw. He rocked back, nearly falling over but catching himself on the edge of the kitchen bar.

He started to surge forward again but Kate had locked her knees into place and stood in a perfect shooter's stance less than three feet from him.

"Move and I'll take out your knees," she said.

Neely seemed to think about it for a moment. In the seconds that hung in the air, Kate desperately wanted to take stock of the situation. She was afraid the woman—apparently Mrs. Coleman—would be dead in a handful of moments. She also had no idea how badly DeMarco was injured. She saw DeMarco getting to her feet out of the corner of her eye. Even without taking her eyes away from Neely, she could tell that DeMarco was holding her cut arm close to her body.

"Drop the knife, Jeremy," Kate said. "We know what you did to the other families. Anything you do from this point on is just going to make it worse for you."

He smiled, as if this was great news. And then he swung the knife around in a flash, aimed directly for DeMarco.

Kate lowered her aim and pulled the trigger. The shot took Neely directly above the knee. His leg crumpled as he went to the floor. DeMarco wasted no time in throwing her full weight into his back.

As Kate dropped to her knees to pull his arms back and handcuff him, the policemen who had been waiting at the top of the driveway came rushing through the door with their guns drawn. Kate assumed they'd been alerted by the first gunshot when she'd blasted through the lock.

It couldn't have taken them more than twenty seconds to run down here, Kate thought. *Is that really all the time that passed between now and then?*

"I'm good here for now," Kate said, snapping the cuffs closed. "Get an ambulance out here. We've got a woman in what looked like critical condition, and a wounded FBI agent."

Kate looked at DeMarco to gauge her situation but saw that the younger agent was kneeling down by Mrs. Coleman. Meanwhile, Mr. Coleman was looking around as if in shock. Kate didn't think he had been cut badly enough to the point where his life was in danger, but the ordeal had certainly unglued him.

"Why?"

The question came from the floor, from the mouth of Jeremy Neely.

"Excuse me?" Kate said.

"Why? Why did they not love me?"

For reasons she could not even start to understand, a wave of pity washed through her. She had to turn away from Neely. Instead, she focused on DeMarco. Her left arm was bleeding heavily, the wound located on the backside of her upper arm.

"We need to stop the bleeding," DeMarco said.

"I will," she said. "But we need to help her first."

Mrs. Coleman's eyes were open but they seemed to be looking somewhere very far away, some place on the other side of the ceiling. There was blood everywhere—splashed along her cheeks, covering her chest, on the floor.

"Ruth…"

Her husband was starting to come around. Kate tried to turn her attention to him, to break his focus before he saw the state his wife was in.

As it turned out, she was about half a second too late. Mr. Coleman saw his wife and something inside of him broke. It was a haunting sound that tore through the house even as Kate, DeMarco, and the local officer did what they could to stop Ruth Coleman's bleeding.

The husband's screams were piercing and filled with torment. They filled the house and Kate's head until the sound of approaching sirens and the wails of ambulances drowned him out five minutes later.

CHAPTER THIRTY ONE

Kate sat in the little sterile hospital examination room with DeMarco, looking at her phone. It was 8:55 and she was staring at a blank text screen with Allen's name above it. She had been thinking of what to say for the last minute or so and finally decided on: **So I'm terrible. Work called again. Same case. But we wrapped it. That means no dinner. I'm so sorry.**

She sent it and then looked at DeMarco. She was sitting on the very edge of the little examination bed. There was a gauze wrapping around her left arm where she had been cut. She hadn't lost too much blood and although the wound had been rather deep, it had been easily fixed with sixteen stitches.

"Was that to your daughter?" DeMarco asked.

"No. Boyfriend."

DeMarco nodded with a frown. "It's been rough on you, huh? Trying to balance all of this."

"Yeah. But I'm getting the hang of it. I just have to stop disappointing those around me who live normal lives. And I...wait. Hold on. You're the one that got stabbed in the arm. What the hell are you doing worrying about me?"

DeMarco shrugged and looked at the floor. "My mom used to tell me stories when I was young about how she almost didn't go the family route. She was playing guitar and singing in this band that nearly made it. She told me how she always admired Stevie Nicks...you know, the singer from Fleetwood Mac?"

"Yes, I know who she is."

"Well, my mom looked to Stevie on how to act, how to play the role of a female lead in a band. And oh my God, this is going to come out way cheesier than I intended but...you're my Stevie Nicks, Kate. The moment I made it as an agent back in the Violent Crimes Unit, I started researching your older cases, learning from you and digging through your files. So yes...I am going to worry about you. The fact that you came back out of retirement to do things like we did tonight floors me."

"Thanks for that," Kate said, feeling tears welling up.

If only Melissa thought of me in that same way.

Her phone buzzed in her hand. She looked down and saw that Allen had returned her text. **I understand. Raincheck. Call me when you get in.**

She was relieved that he had taken it so well but she also felt like she was taking advantage of him. She thought about texting Melissa to fill her in but decided against it. Melissa didn't even know she had been called back out to Roanoke anyway. Thinking of them both so closely together, it then occurred to Kate that Melissa didn't even know about Allen.

It can't be a good thing that DeMarco already knows more about my personal life than my own daughter does, Kate thought.

Still slightly reeling from DeMarco's comments, Kate tried to think of something equally sentimental to tell DeMarco, but was interrupted by a knock at the door. After a second or two, it opened and Palmetto walked in.

"How's it going?" he asked.

"DeMarco is a hero," Kate said, using that as her return compliment.

"Sixteen stitches does not make me a hero," DeMarco argued. "Although it does add a scar and scars are sort of badass."

"I'm just glad it wasn't worse. You truly did save the day, Agent DeMarco. So thanks for that."

"Anyway, I just wanted to drop by and fill you guys in," Palmetto said. "Neely confessed to all of it. He's blaming it on everyone's inability to love him as a child. When they searched him, they found a scrap of the blanket in his back pocket. He openly admitted that it had been intended to go down Ruth Coleman's throat. He said he got the idea from watching his dad kill his mom so easily, like it was nothing. First reactions from the cops are that he's likely going to go for an insanity plea."

"You think he'll get it?" Kate asked.

"Beats me."

"Why the blanket, though?" DeMarco asked.

"That's where more of the crazy comes in. He says it was the only thing he had as a kid that made him feel safe and comfortable. But as he got older and saw how these people who were supposed to love him didn't love him the way he thought they should, the blanket started to take on this whole new meaning. He hated it. Wanted to use something he had once thought of as safe to aid in the murders."

"That's terrible," DeMarco said.

"As for Ruth Coleman, she lost a lot of blood and there were two major arteries that were nicked. One stab wound missed her heart by less than an inch. She also has a punctured lung. She's listed as being in critical condition, but I spoke with the doctor that oversaw her when she came in. It may not be as hopeless as her appearance makes it seem."

"That's fantastic news," Kate said.

"It is," Palmetto agreed. He then looked at DeMarco and said: "Do you mind if I steal Agent Wise away for a second?"

"Not a problem," DeMarco said.

Palmetto opened the door and led Kate out into the hall. He started walking slowly forward and had a thoughtful look on his face.

"What is it?" Kate asked. "Is everything okay?"

"Yes, the case is basically wrapped thanks to you two. But I had something else...something I needed to ask you. I know you're from out of DC and all but I figured it couldn't hurt to ask if you wanted to try to grab dinner or something before you headed back."

It was totally unexpected and she supposed the look on her face said as much. Palmetto's look of thoughtfulness turned to one of apology as she looked for the right words to use.

"Sorry," Palmetto said. "I noticed there's no ring on your finger. I thought it would be okay to ask."

"Oh, it is. And I'm flattered but I'm seeing someone back home. And honestly, between you and I, even if I wasn't, I don't know that I would. My life is sort of a mess right now. There's a balance I need to find and..."

"What?"

"Nothing," she said with a chuckle. "I nearly just dumped a whole lot of complaining on you."

"That would have been okay."

"As for the dinner, I'll have to decline. But seriously...thanks for asking. Sometimes that's all a woman needs to feel worthwhile."

"You're pretty incredible, Agent Wise. I don't see you as having issues with feeling like you're worthy."

If she didn't have Allen back at home waiting for her, she would have kissed him right there and then. Not out of an attraction or strong desire but because those were pretty close to the exact words she'd needed to hear ever since pulling herself out of the dark period she'd lived through after her husband, Michael, had been killed.

"Thank you," Kate said. "For the comments and your help on the case."

He nodded, understanding that her comment had ended the talk of relationships and placed them back on official business. "It was a pleasure meeting you, Agent Wise. DeMarco, too. Be safe getting back home."

With that, he continued down the hallway. Kate watched him go for a while before heading back to DeMarco. When she returned to the room, the nurse had returned and was handing DeMarco the outpatient paperwork.

"What did Palmetto want?" DeMarco asked, looking up from the forms.

"Nothing."

"Everything good?"

Kate smiled. She looked at DeMarco's arm. She thought of Melissa, Michelle, and Allen back at home. She thought of the Colemans, both together and alive elsewhere within this very same hospital.

"Yeah," Kate said with a genuine smile. "Everything is good."

***

After they left the hospital, Director Duran had called to touch based and requested that Kate come back to DC for a brief meeting. She had been looking forward to getting back to Allen as soon as she could but agreed to make the trip. That was how she ended up taking the elevator up to Duran's office on Monday afternoon. Part of her was very nervous, wondering if perhaps she had crossed some lines or had overstepped her bounds in catching Jeremy Neely.

Could be some sort of a complaint or grievance that was filed against me during this last case, she thought. Then, behind that thought came another: *Where is all of this negativity coming from? You never questioned yourself this much before you retired...*

"Agent Wise, welcome back. I'm glad you and Agent DeMarco made it back relatively unscathed. Have you spoken to DeMarco today?"

"I have. She thinks it's ridiculous that she's having to stay at home for a week because of a nick on her arm."

Duran smiled. "You know, Agent DeMarco reminds me of another agent that I know rather well."

"She's much smarter and braver than me," Kate said.

"So you like her as an agent?"

"I do. If I didn't know the situation and you told me she'd only been with the bureau for a little over two years, I wouldn't believe you."

Duran tapped his fingers anxiously on the folder in front of him and slid it over to Kate. "Take a look at this and let me know what you think."

She took the folder and opened it up; there were only two pages inside. And within five seconds of skimming the top one, she understood what she was looking at. She looked up at Duran, making sure he wasn't playing a joke on her.

"Reinstatement?" she asked.

"It's the closest we could come up with based on the fact that you retired. You did not quit and you were not fired. But we also wouldn't be hiring you as a new employee. So yes...consider this the bureau's official request that you come back as a full-time agent. And based on what you've told me today, I'd like to enlist Agent DeMarco as your full-time partner."

Kate looked the forms over and was filled with the same emotions she'd felt when Palmetto had so generously complimented her in the hospital hallway. It made her feel valued. It made her feel wanted.

But she knew she couldn't. Could she?

"I can't move back to DC," she said. "I'm in Richmond for the long haul. My family is there...a new granddaughter and everything."

"We can work around that," he said. "It's not just me, Agent Wise. Even those above me think you're still a valuable asset. I know lots of agents retire and come back to help with research and teaching. And while you'd be great at that, your skills would also be going to waste. I felt it when I was there at the meeting last week where you guided those younger agents towards an answer in the child abduction case—an answer, I might add, that led to an arrest this morning."

She sighed and closed the folder. "Can you give me some time to think it over?"

"Absolutely. Take your time. And again, I truly do appreciate the work you've put in for these last two cases."

"Thanks."

"That's all for now," Duran said. "Sorry to make you come back to DC for this brief meeting."

"It's okay," she said, gripping the edges of the folder. "It was worth it."

CHAPTER THIRTY TWO

It was the first time she'd made pesto from scratch and Kate did not mind saying that it was damned good. She poured it from her pot into a ceramic bowl and placed it on the table by the salad. The entire house smelled of baked ziti and garlic bread. Her back door was open, the screen door allowing a breeze inside. As she stood at the table, making sure she had not missed a beat, the breeze that came through froze her for a moment.

I'm happy here, too, she thought.

She smiled and went to the wine rack in the kitchen. She plucked one bottle of white and one bottle of red from the rack. She set them down on the table just as someone knocked on her front door.

"Come in!" she called.

The door opened and Allen came walking through. He was carrying a small plastic bag and a six-pack of beer. He hefted it up and shrugged. "I didn't know if this was a wine sort of thing or a beer sort of thing."

"Both is fine," Kate said.

She met him at the door, took the plastic bag, and gave him a kiss on the lips. It was a quick one, but Allen took her by the arm with his now-free hand and pulled her back to him. He kissed her again, this time lingering. When they pulled apart, Kate found herself pleasantly dizzy.

"Honestly," Allen said, "I brought the beer for me. I figure if the conversation gets awkward, I can sneak off, chug two of them, and come back in a much looser mood."

"I don't think that will be necessary," she said and then gave a little smirk. "You're meeting my daughter and granddaughter...not my parents."

"That's true, I guess. Still..."

"Why don't you go ahead and start on one now and we'll see how it goes."

"Yes ma'am," he said, taking one of the beers out and popping the top off. "Anything I can do for you?"

"Wine glasses. In the cupboard."

Allen set about helping her, getting the glasses and then taking the cupcakes out of the plastic bag he had brought. He'd gotten them because Kate had told him that Melissa had a soft spot for cupcakes.

"You going to tell her about the offer your director gave you?" Allen asked.

"I think I am," Kate said as she took the ziti out of the oven. "She'll be fine with it. I want to tell her and her husband about it so we can all work together and find out some way that I can balance it all."

Before Allen could respond, there was another knock at the door. This time, it opened without Kate answering. Melissa and Terry stepped inside, Terry carrying Michelle on his shoulder. He took two steps in and his eyes grew wide.

"Man oh man, it smells delicious in here!"

Kate walked over to relieve Terry of Michelle. The baby went to her without any fuss, giving a little smile of recognition. When Kate offered Michelle her finger, the baby took it and gave a little squeeze.

"Sorry," Melissa said as she approached Allen. "My mother sees Michelle and the world just fades out. I'm Melissa."

Allen extended his hand and they shook. "I'm Allen. I've heard a lot about you *and* Michelle, so it's finally nice to meet you."

Terry was next, shaking hands with Allen. Allen offered Terry a beer, which Terry accepted, and that was just about all it took for the two of them to break the ice.

Kate walked back into the kitchen with her granddaughter in her arms. Melissa and Terry were asking Allen several questions, none of which were too pressing or private. Kate joined in as Michelle started swatting at her chin with her chubby little hands.

"You guys ready to eat?" she asked.

"It looks amazing, Mom," Melissa said. "Thanks."

As they all took their seats, Allen passed by her and planted a quick kiss on her cheek. It felt natural. It felt nice and comfortable. She saw that Melissa had seen this and was smiling at her.

Yeah, this is worth keeping, she thought. *This is worth fighting for balance.*

The truth of the matter was that her job fulfilled something within her that her family did not. It seemed like an ugly truth, but it was still the truth. But it had taken her this long, after losing a husband and continuously straining her relationship with Melissa, to understand that the opposite was also true.

Her family offered something that her job never could. Love, support, and a sense of home that came with no goals or expectations.

Kate fully grasped that now. And she knew that she could learn to balance it all.

And with that balance, perhaps she could even be a better agent.

Of course she was going to take Duran up on his offer. She could deny it all she wanted, but she was an FBI agent to her core—and would be until she was a bedridden old lady.

As far as Kate Wise was concerned, she was no longer going to look back on her career with nostalgia and longing.

She had not put it all behind her after all.

IF SHE RAN
(A Kate Wise Mystery—Book 3)

"A masterpiece of thriller and mystery. Blake Pierce did a magnificent job developing characters with a psychological side so well described that we feel inside their minds, follow their fears and cheer for their success. Full of twists, this book will keep you awake until the turn of the last page."
--Books and Movie Reviews, Roberto Mattos (re Once Gone)

IF SHE RAN (A Kate Wise Mystery) is book #3 in a new psychological thriller series by bestselling author Blake Pierce, whose #1 bestseller Once Gone (Book #1) (a free download) has received over 1,000 five star reviews.

55 year old FBI agent Kate Wise is called back in from retirement when a second husband from a wealthy suburb is found murdered, shot to death on his way home. Can it be a coincidence?

There was one case that has haunted Kate her entire career, the one that she couldn't solve.

Now, 10 years later, a second husband is killed in the same way—and from the same, exclusive town.

What is the connection?

And can Kate redeem herself, and solve it before it goes cold again?

An action-packed thriller with heart-pounding suspense, IF SHE RAN is book #3 in a riveting new series that will leave you turning pages late into the night.

Book #4 in the KATE WISE MYSTERY SERIES will be available soon.

Blake Pierce

Blake Pierce is author of the bestselling RILEY PAGE mystery series, which includes thirteen books (and counting). Blake Pierce is also the author of the MACKENZIE WHITE mystery series, comprising nine books (and counting); of the AVERY BLACK mystery series, comprising six books; of the KERI LOCKE mystery series, comprising five books; of the MAKING OF RILEY PAIGE mystery series, comprising three books (and counting); of the KATE WISE mystery series, comprising two books (and counting); of the CHLOE FINE psychological suspense mystery, comprising two books (and counting); and of the JESSE HUNT psychological suspense thriller series, comprising three books (and counting).

An avid reader and lifelong fan of the mystery and thriller genres, Blake loves to hear from you, so please feel free to visit www.blakepierceauthor.com to learn more and stay in touch.

BOOKS BY BLAKE PIERCE

A JESSIE HUNT PSYCHOLOGICAL SUSPENSE SERIES
THE PERFECT WIFE (Book #1)
THE PERFECT BLOCK (Book #2)
THE PERFECT HOUSE (Book #3)

CHLOE FINE PSYCHOLOGICAL SUSPENSE SERIES
NEXT DOOR (Book #1)
A NEIGHBOR'S LIE (Book #2)

KATE WISE MYSTERY SERIES
IF SHE KNEW (Book #1)
IF SHE SAW (Book #2)

THE MAKING OF RILEY PAIGE SERIES
WATCHING (Book #1)
WAITING (Book #2)
LURING (Book #3)

RILEY PAIGE MYSTERY SERIES
ONCE GONE (Book #1)
ONCE TAKEN (Book #2)
ONCE CRAVED (Book #3)
ONCE LURED (Book #4)
ONCE HUNTED (Book #5)
ONCE PINED (Book #6)
ONCE FORSAKEN (Book #7)
ONCE COLD (Book #8)
ONCE STALKED (Book #9)
ONCE LOST (Book #10)
ONCE BURIED (Book #11)
ONCE BOUND (Book #12)
ONCE TRAPPED (Book #13)
ONCE DORMANT (book #14)

MACKENZIE WHITE MYSTERY SERIES
BEFORE HE KILLS (Book #1)
BEFORE HE SEES (Book #2)
BEFORE HE COVETS (Book #3)
BEFORE HE TAKES (Book #4)
BEFORE HE NEEDS (Book #5)

BEFORE HE FEELS (Book #6)
BEFORE HE SINS (Book #7)
BEFORE HE HUNTS (Book #8)
BEFORE HE PREYS (Book #9)
BEFORE HE LONGS (Book #10)

AVERY BLACK MYSTERY SERIES
CAUSE TO KILL (Book #1)
CAUSE TO RUN (Book #2)
CAUSE TO HIDE (Book #3)
CAUSE TO FEAR (Book #4)
CAUSE TO SAVE (Book #5)
CAUSE TO DREAD (Book #6)

KERI LOCKE MYSTERY SERIES
A TRACE OF DEATH (Book #1)
A TRACE OF MUDER (Book #2)
A TRACE OF VICE (Book #3)
A TRACE OF CRIME (Book #4)
A TRACE OF HOPE (Book #5)

9 781640 296893